THE
EASY
OUT

THE EASY OUT

BY JOE ARCHIBALD

Macrae Smith Company
Philadelphia

THE
EASY
OUT

● ONE

UTILITY INFIELDER FRANK HYATT, ONLY FOUR DAYS UP from Denver, of the Pacific Coast League, sat on the Milwaukee Chiefs' bench and focused envious eyes on the big youngster who was digging in at the plate for the St. Louis Redlegs, wishing he could reach back and use at least half a dozen of his years over again. Pete Ibarra, the number two Milwaukee catcher, shifted his chew from one side of his face to the other and said, "Twenty years old and hitting over three hundred in his sophomore year. It took me eight years to hit over two-eighty."

Sam Kelso, the Chiefs' manager, went to the top step of the dugout and waved Martsell, his picket man in right, closer to the foul line, for Tallwood was a murderous pull-hitter. There was one man out and a Redleg base runner waiting to be picked up at second. His eyes half shut, Frank watched Bob Overgaard, the Milwaukee right-hander, fire a pitch in that brushed the hitter back. The count ran to two balls and one strike. Overgaard tried to jam the hitter, but got behind three and one. Looking for a chance to make a double play, Kelso quickly ordered his pitcher to put Tallwood on. It was the top of the seventh and the Chiefs were hanging on to a slim, one-run lead. Turnbull, the Redleg shortstop, stepped in to hit, and Overgaard let him wait. He wiped the sweat off his brow, hitched at his pants, rubbed the ball up, then went to the rosin bag. The crowd and the St. Louis bench prodded him.

The Milwaukee bench fired verbal tomahawks back at the visitors, but the player up from the minors kept his lips tight, for he was little more than a stranger here. For the most part the Chiefs had been passably friendly toward him, particularly the weathered veterans who were about ready to take the trail down the other side of the mountain. It said on the scorecards that he was Frank Hyatt, wearing number 26, and was a utility infielder. It did not say that he was pushing twenty-nine or why it had taken him so long to arrive at a major league ball park. As if anybody cared.

Overgaard tried to keep his pitches around Turnbull's knees to get the man to hit the ball on the ground, but he got two pitches too low, and one that made the batter skip rope. Kelso went out to the mound, where he was joined by his catcher, Al Jansky, and his first baseman, Ira Eckert. The fickle crowd wanted Kelso to bring in a fireman. The umpire wanted the game to go on, and he came out on the grass and angrily told the Milwaukee pilot to make up his mind. Kelso slapped Overgaard on the back, threw a few words at the man in blue, and then strode back to the dugout.

Frank Hyatt's eyes, meanwhile, had been sweeping the far reaches of the Milwaukee stadium. Compared with the baseball plants he had worked in for so many years, this playing area seemed the size of the field where they had fought the Battle of Gettysburg. Even the base lines looked twenty feet longer than those out in the bush. Abstractedly he watched Turnbull take the automatic strike, and then the hitter swung at Overgaard's three and one pitch and slammed a double to the right field corner. When Martsell had trouble fielding the ball, Tallwood raced around with the second run for the Redlegs. Kelso lost no time getting out to the mound, where he took the ball from the tiring right-hander. Overgaard, a man of short temper, fired his glove into the dugout from twenty feet out, and the player up from Denver had to duck. The pitcher said, "Sorry, mister," and continued on to the showers.

Frank turned a grin toward Hy Brown, a reserve outfielder sitting next to him. "I sure hope that was an accident."

"Of course it was, man," the Negro player said. "Bob's just about the friendliest man you'll ever meet. Ask for the shirt off his back and he'll give it to you, no questions asked."

"That would be a switch," Frank said, and the outfielder eyed him from under knitted brows.

"I think I lost you right there, man."

"Forget it." He felt like telling the dusky player that he was the guy who generally stripped the shirt off his back, and that it had caused most of the troubles he had known —that a few friends he had made in the past would have been more useful to him, perhaps, as enemies. He lifted his five feet, eleven inches of spike-scarred anatomy off the bench and went to the drinking fountain, half expecting a rib regarding his slightly bowed legs. Well, he'd tell them that he had not been born that way. The world had knocked his underpinnings into that shape.

Turning away from the fountain, he bumped into Kelso, and the manager snapped irritably, "Watch it," and then slammed his big right fist against the palm of his other hand when his big relief pitcher, Lou Stringham, fired a third strike by the St. Louis hitter.

The southpaw got the next batter to sky to Raneri in center, and the Chiefs came off the field. Kelso shouted, "Let's get some runs. Let's get healthy!"

Eckert, the big first baseman and a three hundred hitter, gave the manager a sour look. "That Winant has all his good stuff today, Sam. He's sure made an invalid out of me."

Picking out his pet piece of lumber, Al Jansky threw over his shoulder, "That ump hasn't been much nourishment, Sam. That last third strike he called against me couldn't have been hit with a mashie." He strode out there, Eckert following. The natives were getting restless and they seemed to demand rather than implore Jansky to hit one out into the picnic area. Twenty thousand of them were in the stands on this steaming hot August afternoon, for the Chiefs were running third in the pennant race and still had an outside chance of overhauling the Pittsburgh Corsairs.

Frank sat in a kind of waking dream, still not fully convinced he had become a major league ballplayer. He dropped his eyes to the script running along the front of his shirt, involuntarily brushed the tips of the fingers of his right hand across the Indian head on the short sleeve of his left arm. Yes, he was here in the flesh and no longer just in his dreams. But he felt like a kid who had arrived late at a lavish birthday party to find most of the refreshments gone. Right now he was sitting a little scared lest Kelso call him for the first time from the seclusion of the dugout.

He tried to look alive and made a feeble attempt to add his voice to the verbal barrage aimed at Billy Winant. The St. Louis fireballer just grinned at the Chiefs' jockeys as he worked at his trade against Jansky. With the count three and two, he gave the catcher a big motion, pulled the string and struck him out. Kelso paced up and down, growling down his rain-barrel. He kicked a towel out of the way, told Hy Brown to pull his big feet in and out of the way. The crowd was beginning to abuse the Chiefs. Eckert, looking for only his second hit of the series, dug in at the left side of the plate and waved his big bat at Winant. "Two out," a fan shouted from a field box.

Frank put himself in Eckert's shoes and his sweat ran freely. A .260 hitting busher facing Billy Winant for his first time at bat in the majors—a juicy target for twenty thousand rabid fans, most of whom would soundly berate their grandmothers if they happened to burn a batch of biscuits. People of ordinary stature and with ordinary accomplishments demanding perfection in others. Up to now he had never performed before more than six thousand spectators. Here the population of a fair-sized city plus millions of TV viewers had you under a microscope as if you were something thrown back from a lost world. All at once he wished he had never cleaned out his locker back in Denver.

Acquiring callouses on the bench, a ballplayer generally lets his mind drift back—especially a journeyman player who has been thrown the last straw. He was, Frank thought, almost like a drowning man reviewing his small sins, his failures, his accomplishments and regrets.

He was eleven years old. A shaggy dog looking on, he sat in an attic room of the Hyatt farmhouse treating a baseball glove with a special oil. He whistled happily through two front teeth that had not as yet quite grown together, for this was a red letter day he had marked on the calendar several weeks ago. The Indiana sky outside was as blue as a robin's egg and seemed to have been made to order for the Little League tryouts over at the county seat. His father had promised him release from work in the fields on this special day.

They were gathering out in the yard, a few of the neighbors' kids, ready to go out to the big strawberry bed and pick the fruit that had ripened since yesterday and carry it to the roadside stand out on the highway. Tom Thorp was going to pick him up at nine o'clock. Tom was part Munsee Indian and had played for Elkhart before the Class A League had been abandoned. The man had taken a lot of time away from his garage to teach the youngsters of White River how the game of baseball had to be played.

Frankie wished the hands of the alarm clock on his dresser would speed up a little. He walked to the wall on his side of the bedroom to straighten out a picture of Stan Musial. He guessed he had the biggest gallery of famous baseball stars in that part of the state. They went back as far as Rube Waddell and Christy Mathewson. He swung his eyes toward his older brother Ben's part of the room. Three photographs adorned that wall, two of them likenesses of Harry James, and one of Satchmo, Louis Armstrong. Ben had decided a few weeks ago that he was going to be a trumpet player, and as usual his whim had been indulged. Frankie, after listening to his brother blow the horn, was certain sweeter music came out of the one attached to the family's old pick-up truck.

He was putting his heavy-soled sneakers and baseball glove in a small nylon bag when he heard the phone ring downstairs, and for some reason he did not like the sound it made. He went out in the hall to listen and heard his mother's voice say, "I'll tell him, and thanks for calling." When he got downstairs his mother was at the front door calling Ben into the house, and when his brother appeared he dropped the nylon bag to the floor, for all at once it seemed to weigh fifty pounds. Something had gone wrong. It was written plainly on his mother's face before she gave Ben the message.

"Mr. DeCarlo called, Ben. He has to go away for two weeks, and if you want to have a lesson before he leaves, it will have to be at ten thirty this morning." She glanced from one of her boys to the other, plainly distressed.

Ben said, "I've been goin' good with the horn lately and I really ought to get that lesson."

"Wait now," Frankie said, "You know Pa won't let both of us off. And I was promised——"

"Sure, I know," Ben said. "I'll forget the trumpet. You go along, Frankie."

The screen door banged open and Matt Hyatt came in and said, "What's holdin' us up, Ben? That stuff is waitin' to be picked." He was a heavy and solid man who had known little save hard work during long hours, and he'd become rigidly practical, and it was not written in his book that the lack of play made Jack or any other kid a dull boy. He listened to his wife for a moment, then nodded his head. "Sure, we promised, Frankie," he said. "So I'll leave it up to you. I can't spare the both of you today because we're two pickers short. Baseball don't pay the taxes on this place, but strawberries do. Seems to me learnin' a musical instrument is more important than throwin' a ball around, though." He went out and slammed the door behind him.

Frankie stewed inside. His father's inference had been plain enough. He was expected to yield, as he always had, to adolescent seniority, and if he rebelled—well, he'd pay, in one way or another. And Ben, standing there waiting, had a disarming countenance. For a fourteen-year-old he could mask his feelings like an expert poker player and he had the knack of coming up with the most subtle reprisals.

A car drove up outside and honked, and Frankie left the nylon bag where it was and went out and told Tom Thorp he wouldn't be going with him. He did not wait to hear the man's reactions but came back into the kitchen, picked up his bag and walked upstairs. Tears stinging his eyes, he fell prone upon his bed and pounded his fists against the pillow. Last year it had been Ben who had gone to the Little League tryouts and hadn't come close to qualifying, and so it looked as if his folks were not aiming to let him outshine Ben. He sat up and stared at the trumpet in its case resting on the table near his brother's bed and he had to fight off the urge to go over there and twist it into the shape of a pretzel. Ben came in, pulling his work shirt up over his head. "You could have gone, Frankie. I didn't say——"

"Shut up!" Frankie said, and balled his little fists. "You don't have to say. You know all the time how miserable they'd make it for me if I crossed you."

"Look, you wouldn't have a chance over there against that bunch to make the Muncie team. Believe me, I know. What can you get out of baseball, Frankie? I could get with a combo in high school and maybe make some money playing at dances and——"

"You?" Frankie shouted as he peeled off his good

clothes. "One of our pigs out there in the pen could play that horn better. I'm hopin' maybe you'll blow your brains out on that thing."

Ben Hyatt gave his brother that maddening surface smile, and assumed an expression of tolerance. "Sure, Frankie, I don't blame you for getting sore. I'll make it up to you."

Frankie pulled on his sweatshirt over his dungarees and got ready to head for the strawberry bed. "Like I told you before, Ben, I wish I'd been born an orphan!"

═══════════

A great explosion of sound brought him back to the Milwaukee stadium with a jolt. It thinned to a long-drawn-out groan when the long ball off Eckert's bat curled foul. The count even at two and two, Winant threw his change-up and the batter watched it go by for a ball. The Redleg catcher spun around and jawed at the umpire and missed being banished from the game by just one word.

Eckert, Frank thought, did not look his thirty years as he guarded the plate, possibly because he had made it big from the start, and had suffered through the minimum of bus rides, greasy food and lumpy beds. Just before he had suited up, he'd looked at his own face in the mirror next to his locker, and the image had been disturbing. There were signs of crow tracks at the corners of his dark eyes, and parentheses at each corner of his mouth. His dark hair, he thought, was beginning to retreat back from his forehead. He grinned down at his feet. By his face, he mused, nobody would ever believe he had been weaned a little too late on the milk of human kindness.

The fans came to their feet again when Eckert got

15

hold of Winant's fast ball and rode it high and far to right. It looked for a moment as if it might go all the way, but it suddenly faded and was gloved by the St. Louis picket deep on the warning track. Eckert put on the brakes between first and second and kicked up a cloud of dust. As he approached the Milwaukee dugout a certain loud-mouth in a nearby box got on him hard and he suddenly made a dash for the railing. Hy Brown was the first Chief off the bench, yelling for Frank to follow him. The dusky outfielder grabbed Eckert around the hips just as the first baseman tried to vault the railing, and Frank caught at one of his arms and held on.

Kelso and nearly a dozen players moved in, along with a pair of stadium police, and Eckert was finally contained. "You fat mouth!" Johnny Drew, the Chiefs' third sacker, ripped at the frightened fan. "I'll bet you beat your wife!" Boos showered down on the field box, and somebody threw a seat cushion. Hundreds of voices blended in a request that the customer get himself out of the stadium.

Eckert, contrite, took his place on the bench and opined that he ought to fine himself fifty dollars. "The slump has me down, Sam," he said to Kelso, and made his way to the drinking fountain. He stopped and looked at Frank. "Thanks, Hyatt. You get an assist."

"About time I earned my pay," Frank said, adding a wry smile. The recognition made him feel much better, as if he belonged, after a fashion. He turned his attention to the action and winced at the sharp impact of Winant's fast ball into the mitt of the Redleg receiver. The pitch blew right past Martsell and the count on the board said two strikes and one ball. One thought was consoling: If hitters of the stature of Jansky and Eckert couldn't hit Winant, would even the most demanding fan expect miracles from a busher?

16

Martsell looked at a slider that caught the outside corner of the plate, and walked away, firing his protective helmet toward the Milwaukee batboy. While the Redlegs came in from the field, a fan high in the stands blew a horn. It startled him as if he had been poked in the ribs. It sent his mind wandering again. The past, he had heard somewhere, never really stayed buried but remained a part of the present and could have a bearing on the future, and while there were such things as dreams and memories you could throw away all the clocks and calendars. Time was *now*, especially for aging ballplayers.

There was a new breed taking over now, and it almost seemed that ballplayers were bought, not made. They no longer came out of the mines and the factories, but out of the high educational mills with all kinds of degrees. They sure had a big jump on players like himself, the sandlot kids.

TWO

FRANK WATCHED RICHIE DUHAMEL, THE CHIEF'S SECOND
baseman, leave the on-deck circle and trot out to his
position, where he immediately began to chatter like a
big-lunged jaybird. Duhamel had been with the Chiefs
for over ten years and was beginning to slow down a
little—had become accident-prone—but his knowledge
of National League hitters compensated for the speed
and the range he had lost. A stick of type in a newspaper
a few days ago had said Frank Hyatt had been brought up
from Denver just in case.

Lou Stringham could not find the plate with his breaking stuff. With the count three and one against him he
fired the fast one in too fat, and the Redleg shortstop,
Turnbull, lined a single to left. When Joe Arriga seemed
to loaf coming in on the ball, Turnbull put on a burst of
speed and tried for two. Arriga's bullet throw was on a

line to Duhamel, and the runner was out by a foot despite a desperate hook slide. The Redleg was limping as he walked back to the visitors' dugout. Pete Ibarra grinned and said, "I'll bet that's a sweet strawberry he's got on his hip."

The remark took Frank back to that little Indiana farm once more where he had developed an aversion to strawberries even when smothered in cream. As far as he was concerned they were bitter fruit, for they always bloomed and ripened when baseball was in the ascendancy. They had kept him out of the Little League. He had never even seen a Little League game. They had made him come up the hardest way, via cow pastures and isolated sandlots.

He looked out at Arriga, backing up to get under a towering fly at the warning track, and he guessed those fruit beds his father had set out every year would have covered most of that outfield. That horn blew again and turned one corner of his mouth up. Strawberries and a brass trumpet. Could there ever have been a more incongruous double-play combination to cut a man down? The last time he had seen Ben's horn was when he'd helped clean out the attic before the family quit the hardscrabble farm and moved to Muncie. It represented a story older than the hills: Make way for the first-born, for his rank has its privileges.

Stringham walked the opposing pitcher, Winant, committing the cardinal sin, and Kelso hopped to the top step of the dugout. When the Redleg leadoff man, Burger, rapped a single through the middle, the manager took the walk to the mound and lost no time signaling to the bullpen. Another southpaw took the long stroll in and Stringham's jaws worked feverishly on a wad of gum as he came to the bench. The man's eyes told Frank that the job of staying in the big leagues was just as tough, if not tougher, than getting there. Stringham complained, "Sam, I could have hung in there!"

"What's the difference between getting hung and getting your brains knocked out, Lou?" Kelso turned his back on the pitcher and watched his fireman, Zach Izzro, throw in his warmup pitches. During the delay Frank mentally took a stroll back over the long road that led back to the bushes. He had made up his mind that he would never be able to leave the past alone.

One of the few breaks he'd ever had was when his father decided to quit farming and take a job in an auto parts factory in the city. It afforded him the chance to play high school ball, at least for two years, and then in April of his Senior year with a wealth of material at the coach's disposal he found that he had to give himself up again. True, he had been given a choice, but one that had him stymied. A week after practice began he had found himself battling a transfer student from upstate for the second base position, and had no qualms as to his ability to survive the competition until made aware of a less than fortuitous combination of circumstances.

He would never forget the day his father had put it right on the line. "It happens to be this way, Frank," he had said. "That kid's father was brought here to take over as foreman in the department where I work. He didn't come right out and say it, of course, but he let me know his heart's set on his kid making a reputation as a ballplayer in high school so's he can catch on with a college team. He asked me if I was sending any kids of mine to college. I know what he meant even though he thinks I might look dumb. There could be some layoffs at the plant and if you beat that kid out . . ."

Frank had understood, all right. He had to realize what side the family bread was buttered on, and so he had deliberately missed the next two practice sessions. The kid from upstate was at second base when the first league game was played, and Frank Hyatt had watched from the bench. He'd stayed there most of his Senior year.

College? Ben had been the one to go, and he'd come home halfway through his sophomore year admitting he could go just so far with the textbooks. And Matt Hyatt had been convinced that if Ben couldn't make it his younger son surely couldn't, with a mind that was generally on baseball.

After that the road had been rocky and all uphill, and while going from job to job he had just about given up the game of baseball, until Tom Thorp organized a four-team Industrial Sunset League where he played three games each week for the Felch Wire & Cable Company. It had paid off only with experience.

———

The present came back to him in the shape of a hard baseball driven straight into the Milwaukee dugout by Rocca, the Redleg center fielder. The ball missed his head by a couple of inches and bounced back onto the field. Izzro laughed at his bench, then looked in at Jansky for the sign. His next two pitches were wide of the plate, and the crowd began to squirm; for waiting in the on-deck circle, swinging three bats, was Ted Cryner, third in the league in the matter of home runs. The fans cheered when Rocca took a second strike, and then became pan-

21

icky when Izzro threw one in low that made the batter dance a jig. They screamed for Kelso to get Zach out of there just as Rocca took a full cut and popped the ball high back of first, where Eckert easily gathered it in. The pitcher, something of a comedian, responded to a round of applause with an exaggerated tip of his cap. Then he spat into the dirt.

Kelso gave Izzro a hard look. "Public relations, Sam?" the pitcher said. "I don't have even one in the stands."

Frank bought Zach's observation. All those people that came out to see baseball—how would they know how it feels out here when the pressure is on, what it does to a man? Who are they to tell you how to play this game—the butchers, the bakers, the brokers, the salesmen and the stenographers? They paid for the privilege, along with the peanuts and hot dogs, to scream bloody murder when an error was made, or to go into hysteria when a ball reached the seats. One minute their thumbs were up and then they were down, demanding a man's baseball life. Sure, he had had relations with the public all the way from the sandlots and Class A ball. He would take vanilla.

Duhamel was out there waggling a bat at Billy Winant, and a fan from back of first yelled, "Bunt it, you bum! Or let it hit you in the seat!"

"See what I mean, Sam?" Izzro tossed at Kelso.

The St. Louis third baseman and first sacker moved in on the grass with Winant's first pitch, and Duhamel shortened up and fouled it off. That horn up in the high seats blew again, and it reminded Frank that he should answer Ben's last letter and tell him he was sorry but he was short of money himself and that he'd have to get a loan at the bank. Winant got his second offering across Duhamel's knees, and then he cut loose with his fast one that Duhamel ignored. The Redleg catcher fired the ball to his third baseman, and the batter turned and walked toward the bench, his ears coloring up in the face of the crowd's belaboring.

Kelso let Izzro hit, and a few moments later he was Winant's ninth strikeout victim. The fans turned on Kelso, wanting to know if he had such a thing as a bench. What was he saving Hy Brown and Ibarra for? Next year's World Series? And where was that banjo hitter the Chiefs had called up from Denver?

Frank was not sure where he was himself, or why. As the Chiefs took the field he wondered if he might be trade bait, for there were only about four weeks to go. Up to now he had not even been called upon to run for a man and he felt as if he was something scraped off the bottom of the barrel. Bert Moger, the Denver pilot, must have sold the parent club a real bill of goods. Apparently Bert had a soft spot in his leathery old heart for stray cats and dogs and itinerant ballplayers. He must not forget to send the manager a box of his villainous cigars when he got his pay check.

"It'll look kind of big and scary to you up there at first," Moger had said when they had shaken hands goodbye, "but as soon as you throw your first man out and get that first hit, it'll all drop into normal perspective. Blow this chance, Frank, and you're dead and they'll take you back to Class AA and bury you."

Never, Bert! he told himself as the St. Louis leadoff man came up for the top of the ninth.

Izzro had two heavy lumbermen, Cryner and Mc-Tigue, to get past before the Redleg batting order dwindled in power. He fell behind on Cryner, two and nothing, and then sent the batter sprawling with a fast ball inside. Kelso put in a distress call to his bullpen, and moved to the top step of the dugout. Cryner took the automatic strike and then got the green light and creamed a slider to the left field corner and reached second standing up. A lot of the die-easy fans began moving toward the runways and one shouted as Jansky went out to settle Izzro down, "Tell him to walk McTigue, Al, then pick him off first!"

The Chiefs' southpaw bowed his neck and made McTigue hit his pitch, a sinker that the batter slammed right at Johnny Drew at third, who took it on one hop and fired it to Eckert for the first out. Watching Izzro out there, standing in his sweat, going through all the nervous motions characteristic of pitchers, Frank counted one blessing, for he might have been a pitcher, and in that fraternity the mortality rate was high. Out there in the bullpen Danny Sloat was throwing—a man with a status almost as shaky as his own.

The St. Louis hitter fouled Izzro's first pitch out of the stadium, got fooled by a change-up, then skied deep to Martsell, Cryner going to third after the catch. Movement in the stands slowed down, and Izzro took a long, deep breath as the pressure fell away from him. Enshaw, the St. Louis pilot, made his move here, sending up a right-handed hitter to face Kelso's southpaw, and a terrific burst of applause came out of the stands when Izzro bore down and struck the pinch hitter out.

Kelso slammed his pitcher on the back, clapped his hands at the Chiefs following Izzro into the dugout. "Let's tie it and finish it here," he shouted. "It's too hot for extra innings."

The top of the batting order would face Billy Winant. First Ken Provost, then Johnny Drew, to be followed by Cal Raneri. If one should get on, Joe Arriga would get his cut.

24

Frank leaned back and folded his arms across his chest, content in a way to postpone his debut for yet another day, at the same time wishing it might be otherwise. He was like a man who went to the high diving board for the first time wanting to take off but was wary of making the try. He suddenly leaned forward when Winant missed with his first two pitches and caught himself shouting along with the other Chiefs for Provost to hang in there. Kelso shot a glance his way, a small grin wrapped around it. The manager shouted above the clamor of the fans, "That's it, Hyatt. Stay alive!"

His heart hammered his ribs. The remark could have meant that Kelso was considering taking Duhamel out if the game went into extra innings. The veteran keystone man was well over thirty and it was nearly a hundred in the shade in Milwaukee.

The fans wanting his scalp, Winant rubbed up a new ball. He let Provost wait while he checked the St. Louis defensive alignment, sleeved sweat off his face and straightened out a pantleg. Pete Ibarra cupped his big hands over his mouth and yelled out of the home club's tepee, "Fish or cut bait, Billy!"

It was Provost who went fishing. He took a vicious cut at Winant's curve ball that swept far outside, and the fans' reaction reddened the leadoff man's ears. He stepped out, looked up the third base line for the sign, got it, then picked up a handful of dirt. "Throw it in Winant's face, Provost, and get a walk!" a fan shouted as he took a foothold in the batter's box. His infield alert for the bunt, Winant hummed one in knee-high and Provost fouled the ball back. The Redleg ace wasted two pitches, then gave Provost a sinker that registered his tenth strikeout.

Hy Brown sighed deeply. "You can see why they pay

Billy thirty grand a year," he said to no one in particular.

"What does he do with his old clothes?" Frank asked.

"He's my build—just taller. I could shorten the pants."

A murmur of amusement ran the length of the bench, and he felt a touch of embarrassment. Pete Ibarra said, "Yeah, they pay him twenty-nine thousand, five thousand for pitching, the rest for hitting."

Johnny Drew, up there trying to get something going, ran the count all the way out on Winant, then popped up to short. Their team down to the last out, most of the twenty thousand fans were off their seats and moving away. "Get a good pitch, Cal!" Kelso yelled at Raneri as the center fielder stepped to the plate. Winant, the bases clean, went into his jumble of arm and legs windup and turned his fast ball loose, but a moment later he wished he could have taken it back. There was that sound that delights the hearts of the baseball fans—the sound like the crack of a high-powered rifle—and the St. Louis left fielder turned and ran back a few feet, then waved good-bye to the ball as it sailed into the picnic area.

Bedlam shook the stands as Raneri circled the bases, and Frank joined the Chief welcoming party when the slugger came to the dugout. The Chiefs nearly tore the shirt off Raneri's back before they let him settle down on the bench. Out in the middle of the diamond Winant still kicked up dirt. The crowd was still in high gear when Joe Arriga took a big stick to the plate, anticipating icing for the cake, but the Redleg left fielder sent the game into overtime with a sparkling catch of an Arriga drive close to the fence.

When the Chiefs took the field for the first of the tenth Frank felt the need of water, for his throat had tightened up again. Extra innings meant juggling the lineup, and there was a good chance he would get in there in some capacity or another and lose the comforting status of an unknown quantity. The water cooled his throat but failed to contain his building tension. He moved to the other end of the dugout and picked up a fresh towel from the pile, came back with it and forgot to use it. Hy Brown's big white teeth flashed at him. "I know the feeling, man. It was only three years ago. You stay loose. You sit loose, Hyatt."

Working on the tail end of the St. Louis batting order, Izzro got two quick outs and seemed to have the third when Duhamel took a grounder deep in the hole and threw wild to Eckert, the runner getting all the way to second. The St. Louis manager reached for his bench, sending up a pinch hitter, Charlie Behringer, a big league veteran of many campaigns. Jansky went out to the mound to give his pitcher the book on the man. The crowd was assailed by ants once more, its noise run through by an almost audible strumming of nerves.

Stay loose, Hy? Frank chuckled inside. I've been as loose-jointed as a scarecrow since I rode the buses in Class A. Once we got an old school bus and the first day I rode in it I ruined a pair of slacks with peanut butter and jelly.

Izzro concentrated on keeping the ball away from the deadly pull-hitter who always aimed for the right field seats. He fell behind three and one, then got the order to put Behringer on. The crowd sensed disaster again. Hy Brown leaned toward Frank. "That gives Enshaw a problem, man. Does he yank his best pitcher out and send up a hitter? His bench is not deep."

Frank, grateful for the attention, shook his head. Winant, halfway to the plate, was called back, and in the St. Louis dugout another pinch hitter was getting some

27

wood. "I'm only a busher, Hy. This looks like a game of Russian roulette to me."

"Billy was looking for his sixteenth win," Pete Ibarra observed. "He won't be palsy walsy with Enshaw for the next couple of days."

The voice blared out of the public address system, only partially registering above the sound washing out of the stands: ". . . and, gentlemen, your-r-r attention, please! Tannehill, Number-r-r thirr-rty-seven, batting for Winant!"

Ibarra said, "These are the times that try managers' souls—if they have such things."

Kelso turned and grinned at the man. "You can believe it, Pete."

● THREE

TANNEHILL, WHO HAD FALLEN JUST SHORT OF BEING THE
prize rookie of the old circuit the year before, was a young
and strong right-handed hitter with a .276 batting average. He sprayed his hits to all fields. He nailed Izzro's
first offering deep to left, the ball curling outside the foul
pole at the last breathless second. Jansky went out to
confer with his pitcher and the tension stretched tight
once more. The chips were down. Either Kelso or Enshaw had guessed wrong.

Hy Brown said to Frank, "I saw two more hairs on
Kelso's head turn gray."

Izzro, ready to work again, drew in a deep breath. He
served one up to Tannehill with a string attached, and
the batter popped it up to short right. Duhamel raced out
and Martsell ran in, and the Chiefs in the dugout and on
the field shouted for the second baseman to keep off. The

Redleg base runners, with two out, were on the move, the lead man barreling around third. Neither fielder gave ground, and Martsell made a miraculous catch as he crashed into Duhamel. The crowd's burst of applause snapped off when the Chiefs' second baseman struggled vainly to get to his feet.

Tom Shugrue, the Milwaukee trainer, hurried out there, Kelso at his heels. Shugrue waved half a dozen players away from Duhamel and bent over the injured player. A few minutes later Duhamel came off the field supported by Eckert and the trainer, a whiteness showing through the tan on his sweaty face. His teeth were clamped tight when they eased him to the bench and applied cold towels. Frank heard Shugrue say to Kelso, "His knee got bumped. Along with his ribs. Can't tell if it's serious until I get him on the table."

It suddenly occurred to Frank as they took Duhamel to the dressing room that the moment of truth for him had arrived. Jansky, Eckert and Martsell were the first three hitters. If one got on, somebody would hit for Duhamel. Jansky stirred the crowd with a sharp single to center, and Frank's blood tingled. When Eckert fanned and Martsell went to the plate, Kelso said in his gravelly voice, "Get yourself a bat, Hyatt!"

The Chiefs gave him words of encouragement as he left the dugout and moved to the waiting station, but they failed to penetrate. Feeling the pressure of thousands of eyes, he was as jittery as a rabbit caught in the glare of an automobile's headlights as he absently picked up the batter's rosin bag. Already the men on the St. Louis bench were sharpening their spurs, and he desperately reached back for Bert Moger's parting words and thought of the struggle he had made to get where he was. The memories of some of the hardest lumps drained much of the buck fever out of him and replaced it with a grim determination that bulged out the muscles of his jaws.

He talked to himself. That Sallee, that pitcher who had taken up Winant's burden, did not look so big out there. In fact, Frank, he's almost the spitting image of a guy you used to hit good in Class AA. You're as tough as the rest of these major leaguers and you have the scars to prove it. If you did not possess most of what it takes, why are you in this ball park? Riding his bat he watched Sallee throw in a two and nothing pitch to Martsell, and a few moments later he was jumping to his feet, watching the ball sail far to right and drop into the seats. The fans were tearing up the proverbial pea patch as Martsell ran out only his third homer of the year, and Frank walked back to the frenzied Milwaukee dugout not sure he was glad or sorry over the reprieve.

"All right, you apes," Martsell said as he peeled off his sodden uniform in the Chief dressing room, "it was strictly Chinese, Ming dynasty, but I'll take as many as I can get."

Baseball, as they said, was a game of inches. One little gust of wind could have carried Martsell's long fly foul, and then the man might have been an out instead of a hero, and he, Frank Hyatt, would have gone to bat for the Chiefs. Danny Sloat, a member of the Milwaukee mound corps in fairly good standing, the player who had split an apartment with Frank on the city's west side, offered him a modicum of sympathy. "I pitched about seventy-two innings in the bullpen, Frank, before Kelso gave me the nod. You got any hair tonic? I'm fresh out."

"Help yourself, Danny. Take the whole bottle. I was only saving it in case they wanted me to demonstrate it on TV." He got up and peeled off the lower half of his uniform just as a Milwaukee writer moved in. Anticipating the man's questions, he said, "I don't know how it feels to be a big leaguer—not yet"—he gave the scribe one of his best grins—"and my folks said I should never talk to strangers." He was sure he had a book on the man's thinking. Here was copy that was a little different, a find like maybe a calf with five legs. A ballplayer without a college degree who had never earned in five years the amount of money a lot of teen-age prospects had received for signing a contract—a man who had arrived in the majors when most players were beginning to think of a plane or train out.

The writer swung an amused glance toward Sloat. "I can't say he's a pop-off, can I?" He turned back to the player up from Denver. "I hope you make it, Hyatt. I really mean it."

"Thanks."

He was nearly finished dressing when Richie Duhamel came out of the trainer's room, favoring his left leg. There was a dark bruise over part of his rib-cage. Martsell hurried toward him and waxed apologetic, and the second baseman good-naturedly waved him off. "I'll be back in a day or two, Herb, unless Hyatt gets hot and steals my job. If that happens, I'll sue you."

Frank grinned into the mirror as he combed his hair, thankful that he had retained his sense of humor. Many people he'd met along the way had accused him of being an incurable patsy. They said that he was too nice a guy at times to ever hope to be a winner. He was his own most friendly enemy. There was very little chance, he knew, of Duhamel's getting into the lineup against the New York Metros tomorrow night, and Kelso had a choice of replacements at the middle station. One of them was just leaving the dressing room with Johnny Drew, and he was a nineteen-year-old kid only a few weeks out of college who had received a bonus of twenty-five thousand dollars. An investment like that, he admitted, could not be left to molder on the bench.

When he arrived at the small apartment with Danny Sloat the phone was ringing and the relief pitcher fairly jumped across the living room to answer it. Frank shed his light sports coat and went to the icebox to get a cool drink, turning a deaf ear to the conversation Sloat was having with what just had to be a girl. Coming back into the room he heard his roomie say, "I don't think there is much chance of that, Kathy, but I'll try. Sure, I'll call you back."

Danny put the phone on its cradle and eyed Frank dubiously. "I know I'm something of a nut to ask, Frank, but how about going out on a double date tonight?"

"Me? Danny, where did your girl meet Dracula's daughter?"

"She isn't fat and she hasn't got buckteeth, Frank. Kathy wouldn't pull a snow job with me. This girl is about your age. A strawberry blonde——"

Frank nearly choked on a swallow of Coke. "Stop right there, Danny. Forget it. The answer is a great big fat no! For one reason, I never was in the position to afford romance, and I never stayed in one place long enough to raise a family if I'd had. You go out and have fun."

"Sure," Danny said. "I'll look for another pinch hitter. Maybe you don't belong in her league anyway."

Frank laughed. "I wouldn't say that, Danny. I've been in them all."

"I shouldn't have said that," the relief pitcher apologized, "but you should try and live a little, Frank. With guys in our profession it is always later than we think."

A half hour later Sloat left the apartment and Frank turned on the TV and got the news while he cooked himself a couple of lamb chops. The sportscaster came on to talk about the game the Chiefs had pulled out in the tenth à la Frank Merriwell, the injury to Duhamel, and the possibility that the fans would see Hyatt, the player up from the Denver farm, in the opener with the Metros. "The Chiefs still have a mathematical chance to win the pennant," the voice out of the picture tube said. "The Quakers beat the Corsairs this afternoon, seven to six. Lorin was knocked out in the second . . ."

Frank shut the TV off, reached for his coat and went out to see what was playing at the neighborhood movie. It was a horse opera he had seen twice before, and he went back to the apartment, stopping on the way to pick up a copy of the *National Sports Gazette,* a publication he had read religiously for years. Always he read "Minor League Highlights" first in order to keep tabs on players he had known, and to see how they were faring. He finally turned a page, two columns of which had been devoted to necrology, and then letters spelling out a certain name became very big and very black in front of his eyes. Eddie Mutino, 31. He skipped a breath, and an ache came up in his throat. That was the number the player had worn at Austin. He read only the first two lines of the obituary, for he knew the story well, and had lived a good part of it.

Salt stung his eyes and he got up and walked to the window and looked out over the rooftops. "So long, Eddie," he whispered. "You'll bat a thousand where you've gone." He could hear the man's laughter, see Eddie's face take shape in the cloud mass rolling in and over the city, and now he felt proud of one sacrifice he had made. He went to the bathroom and splashed cold water on his face, but it did not relieve the lump in his throat. The last he'd read about Eddie was that he was hitting .270 for Oklahoma City.

He went back to his chair by the window, put his head back and closed his eyes. His future doubtful, his present static, a man's mind tends to work in retrospect, and has the capacity to review many hours, days, months, and even years in an incredibly short space of time.

There had been a lot of excitement in the town the night the Felch Wire & Cable team won the Sunset League pennant, for it was the highest-caliber flesh-and-blood baseball available in that neck of the Hoosier woods. Nearly two thousand spectators had turned out, and Frank guessed that nearly half of them tried to tear the uniform off his back when he'd made a dash for his car after belting the winning run home. When he got home he fully expected his father's reaction, and it did not brighten his mood to find Ben there. He knew what Ben's pitch was going to be.

"I'm still not interested, Ben," he said, and started upstairs. "I've got to get that uniform off——"

"Yeah," Matt Hyatt said, "I heard they call 'em monkey suits. They named 'em right. If you had any brains, you'd listen to Ben."

"I've listened to him too many times."

"Look, we're not kids any more," Ben cut in. "We could make a good combo. I got it from the horse's mouth the new highway is going through here, and if we add a lunch counter to the filling station we can clean up."

"How long do you think you'll have a job with Felch, Frank?" Matt Hyatt asked. "You got hired just because you can play ball, and so what happens if you break a leg or an arm? They'll dump you quicker than you can say 'Jackie Robinson.' "

"I have news for you," Frank said. "I might quit *them*. I've got a good chance of playing organized ball, Class A, next summer. Tom Thorp is working on it. He played once with the man who is managing Grand Forks in the Dakota League."

"For peanuts," Ben snorted, "and Ma can expect you to send your laundry home." Ben suddenly made a gesture of resignation and assumed a mien that had paid off many times before, one that had always managed to work for him. "I sure hate to miss the chance of a lifetime," he said, as his mother came in from the kitchen. "Sure, I fouled a couple of things up before, but this time——"

Frank hurried upstairs before he became vulnerable again. There he took a look at his bank book, and it showed a balance of over seven hundred dollars. Getting out of his uniform, he began to wonder if he could leave home early next year with a clear conscience and concentrate on baseball with the knowledge that he'd left bad feelings behind. And Ben was thinking of getting married.

When he went back downstairs Ben was just leaving. "Wait," he said, "I've decided to let you have five hundred dollars, Ben. It's a loan, remember?"

"Sure, Frank. I won't ever forget it."

The expression on his parents' faces was collateral enough for Frank. His mother, seldom a demonstrative woman, gave him a big kiss on the cheek. "Brothers should always help each other," she said, and Frank laughed a little inside for in his case it had always seemed a one-way street.

36

Two weeks later he stopped in to see Tom Thorp, and it happened that the man had received a letter from Grand Forks only an hour before. "It's news both good and bad, Frank," Thorp said. "Like I told you before, things aren't like they used to be. The big leagues load their farms with their own prospects, and as soon as they develop them to a certain degree they yank them. They don't put too big an investment in Class A clubs."

"Let me have it straight, Tom."

"Well, it's this way. Fred Veck wrote that you were welcome to try out with the Bisons next spring at your own expense. It's 'way down in Waycross, Georgia, Frank. If you're good enough to take the second base job away from the candidates they already have, then you'll go on the payroll. Take the chance. It'll be worth it. You were with some pretty fast company in the Sunset League and you hit two–eighty-seven. Comes time and if you need a little money——"

Frank shook his head. "I owe you too much already, Tom. Believe me, I'll swing it."

Thorp nodded. "You will if you think of yourself first, last and always. When it means bread and butter the opposition or the competition will knock you down if they have to. And they won't help you up, Frank."

"I'll remember."

The Milwaukee training complex in the deep south was rougher than he had imagined. He arrived there the first week in March, found himself a room in town, and took a bus out to the area the next morning. At Minor League operations he finally located the Grand Forks pilot. Fred Veck was a short, stubby man who looked on his way past forty. He had worked at a catcher's trade exclusively in the Class AA and Class AAA Leagues.

37

Sun-bleached, bushy eyebrows shaded washed-out blue eyes set unusually wide apart in a weather-toughened, blocky face.

"Glad to see you, Hyatt," he said, shoving a bunch of crooked fingers toward Frank. "You look like you have the makings, kid. The right build, a good pair of hands. The fact you got here tells me you have the right spirit and the guts. Let's go meet some of the others."

In a dressing room on the Minor League side Frank was introduced to over a score of candidates for the Grand Forks club and quickly judged their average age at scarcely twenty-one. They welcomed him politely enough. A few offered their hands, but the majority simply nodded and seemed to be measuring him. Veck said, "All right, move out." Then he turned to Frank and told him to pick an empty locker. "When you're ready," he said, and grinned. "I can't give orders to a man paying his own way. Just instructions."

"I'm buying those," Frank said.

During the days that followed he arrived back at his room bruised both in mind and body. The lowly bushers, especially an eighteen-year-old kid just out of college, also battling for the keystone position, pulled no punches in trying to convince him that nice guys couldn't win. Duke Lubell, holder of the position, told him one afternoon after dumping him sliding into the bag, "You'd better fight back, Hyatt. I'll expect you to do the same to me."

He did not agree with their rough and tumble philosophy. They were forgetting the nice guys like Stan Musial, Joe DiMaggio and Peewee Reese. He played it his way, getting his share of hits, making a minimum of errors and absorbing his lumps without complaint, and when the month of March had almost run out, Fred Veck had him sign a Milwaukee contract. He felt twelve feet tall. He had his foot inside the door of organized baseball. Duke Lubell, who had been shifted to short, was the first to congratulate him. "Maybe I should be giving you sympathy, Frank," he said. "You haven't ridden the Gimpy Goose yet." He threw a broad grin at the Grand Forks manager. "It's an old covered wagon with dead axles, fitted out with a four-cylinder power plant. And the scenery you see from it—the old skulls of buffaloes and the bones of bush league ballplayers."

Nothing, however, dulled the brightness that had come over his world that day, not even a letter from Tom Thorp that said Ben still had not added a stick of lumber to the old building of his filling station but that he'd given his girl a pretty good-sized engagement ring.

They played the other farm clubs working out at Waycross—Boise, Davenport, Eau Claire, and Wellsville— and Frank had a .271 average at the plate when the training grind was over. While the Grand Forks bushers were emptying their lockers, Duke Lubell approached Frank. "Me and Chip Burney drove a jalopy down here. How about joining us and sharing expenses on the way to the Dakotas?"

Six hundred miles out of Georgia Frank discovered there was a reason for Duke's invitation. Both the shortstop and Burney ran short of ready cash, and when the old sedan finally wheezed into Grand Forks, Frank had just about sixty-eight dollars left to his name. And he had a strong hunch that this was one of the times a nice guy was going to lose.

● FOUR

GRAND FORKS, ON THE STORIED RED RIVER, POPULATION close to thirty-thousand, was in the midst of a kind of urban renewal project, and the small apartment building where several of the Bisons bachelors had lived the season before had been renovated and the rents stepped up. "Sure, I understand," Duke said to the man in the rental office. "You're gettin' a better class of people. No more riffraff like ballplayers. Come on, Frank, we must find a home away from home somewhere."

Veck tipped them off to a vacant trailer in a camp just off the campus of the University of North Dakota, and they drove out there, liked it, and took possession. "Not too bad at all," Duke allowed, "if you don't get claustrophobia or don't mind getting jammed when you get to the plate. This isn't a bad town, either. It's got a potato-flour mill, a packing plant and a couple of other industries. But those wide open spaces outside! The biggest hill in the state is where the pitcher stands in the ball park. The kids get to climb it when we're on the road."

"Indiana doesn't remind anybody of Switzerland either," Frank said as he unpacked his bags. He felt another pang of homesickness and tried to put his mother's cooking out of his mind.

Duke stretched out on one of the narrow beds and wondered aloud why he had come back here to start a third year. "I was bright-eyed and bushy-tailed the first year, Frank, and you know I got a crack at Class AAA ball the last part of that season? Couldn't hit curve balls they threw in that league. I was offered a job with a construction company before I left for Waycross this year, running a bulldozer for about one-fifty a week." He laughed. "You know what the payroll of the Bisons is per month? About six thousand, including Veck's pay."

Frank said, "I know."

"I'm going to be twenty-three in a couple of months and if I think then that I'm no better than I ever will be, I'll turn in the monkey suit. Even in the outside world, Frank, they consider men of thirty-five at the peak of efficiency. Lose a job at that age and you're on the scrap heap."

Tom Thorp had given it to him straight, had conditioned him over a year ago, so Duke's pessimism failed to shake him up the least bit, and he'd keep reminding himself that just because his brother Ben had flopped as a trumpet player it did not necessarily follow that he was going to fail as a baseball player. Sure, he knew that Class A players drew little more than three hundred dollars each month, and that they got four dollars for meal money when on the road. Each club was limited to seventeen players and most of the games were played at

41

night on diamonds that were certainly not infielders' best friends. Saturdays were taken up with long bus rides and day games were played only on a Sunday or a holiday.

There would be times, Thorp had said, when there would be no room at the inns and players had to scrounge around for places to sleep. There was no such thing as a road secretary in the remote regions of organized ball, and a man who qualified as a trainer most always found himself at the wheel of the club bus. Class A was baseball's grass roots.

"It isn't too bad on the road," Duke said, getting out of the bed. "They put us up at the best hotels, if possible, but we sleep three in a room"—he grinned—"sometimes four." He picked up the *Grand Forks Record* that was already turned to the sports section. "Five new faces in the lineup," he said. "I'll bet three of them never shaved. Time was when veterans from the majors ended up back here, but no more. This is a cradle for embryonic future stars, not a wheelchair for a has-been."

"Sure, Duke. The big leaguers have a pension plan now."

Three nights later he played his first ball game for pay against the Fargo Blue Sox, the opener drawing nearly five thousand fans, and they set up a racket that would have done credit to twice their number. Sitting on the Bison bench while the Blue Sox took infield practice Frank looked up at the light towers and wondered if a lot of the bulbs were missing or if the Bisons had only paid half of their electric light bill. He was glad he did not have to roam the outfield. Out there the Fargo pickets looked like wraiths as they moved around in the semi-darkness.

Red Quinn was warming up with Veck. The right-hander was only nineteen years old and he had signed with Milwaukee for a bonus of close to ten thousand dollars. "For that dough he quit college," Mose Valentine, the young Negro center fielder, said. "I dunno."

Duke grinned. "Your eyes have turned green, Mose," he said, and drew a bat out of the rack.

The fans clamored for action, for the long Dakota winter had sharpened their hunger for baseball. Fred Veck posed for the cameras with the mayor and then his Honor threw out the first ball. "Let's go," Veck shouted, and Frank, his legs a little unsteady under him, ran out to the field alongside Duke and Mose Valentine. The fans tried out a round of noise for size as the Bisons fired the ball around the infield, and then everybody in the park stood up to a recording of the "Star Spangled Banner."

Duke Lubell talked it up to Red Quinn when the first Fargo batter stepped up to the plate. Frank coughed out some nervousness and leaned over to pick up a pebble that was not there. The hitter cut at Quinn's first pitch and slammed the ball a few feet to his right and he flagged it down back-handed, wheeled and fired to Mike Kaska at first base. The roar of approval from the wooden stands was like a tonic flowing through him. The redhead on the mound seemed to have the poise of a veteran as he cut down the next two Blue Soxers on strikes, and Frank wished that it were possible to buy a small piece of the kid's confidence, even at seven per cent. When the crowd's applause faded, Duke said, "I wonder if those harmonica rascals are——"

The music wafted down from the seats as he picked his bat from the rack—a rendition of "Red River Valley."

"There's three of 'em, Frank," Mose Valentine said to Frank. "Sometimes they play for the local radio station."

Long as they don't play the trumpet, Frank mused.

Fargo threw a southpaw against the Bisons, a rangy youngster who had come to the league late the preceding year. Duke Lubell, leading off, took a strike, then hit the dirt when a high fast one low-bridged him. He got up, brushed himself off, then rode Vic Dente's next offering into right for a single. Frank began to run down the batting order when Lew Monnegan, the left fielder, also hit safely, for it looked as if he'd get his cut the very first inning. Bondi, up there now, would be followed by Kaska, Valentine, and then himself.

Guy Bondi, the big catcher, brought the fans up screaming when he rocketed a three and two pitch over the right field fence, and the Fargo manager lost no time calling in a new pitcher. The right-hander got Mike Kaska, the cleanup batter for Veck, on a high pop-up to the infield, and then Frank moved out to the on-deck station, feeling as if an Indian tom-tom had been planted under his breastbone. The relief pitcher, Degan, got Mose Valentine to hit his sinker on the ground to short and the Negro was out by a step at first.

Frank, almost thankful that no men were on, wiped the moisture off the palms of his hands before he walked to the plate. The Fargo bench worked on him, probing for his most sensitive spots, and the fans in the front seats shouted them down. "Degan beaned a guy last year, Hyatt," the Blue Sox backstop said, "and he still sees double."

"Knock it off, Wes," the umpire said.

"Cold war, ump," the catcher said. "They use it everywhere nowadays."

Degan hummed his fast ball in and Frank took it around the knees. He ran the count even, two and two, then got a pitch he'd always liked, high and a little out-

44

side. He got all the good meat of his bat on the ball and sent a screaming line drive to deep left that the Fargo fielder caught only after a hard run. It was a beginning he would settle for, he thought, as he fired his hard hat away and took over in the field again.

He had a good first night, everything considered. He handled three chances in the field, despite the fact that the ground was hard-packed even so early in the season, and drove out a hit in three official times at bat. The Bisons ground the Blue Sox into the prairie, 12-2. Pitcher-coach Van Lingle won a 4-3 squeaker the following night in eleven innings, Frank going two for five, and the Bismark Senators, pennant winners the year before, checked in at the hotel. After splitting two games, the Bisons got ready to take the long ride to Minot.

"Take a couple of magazines, Frank," Duke Lubell advised the night before the Gimpy Goose was serviced, "and maybe a tranquilizer. It will be no scenic paradise, and after you've ridden the first hundred miles you'll wonder why they didn't let the Indians have it."

"Maybe because there is oil underneath, and millions of dollars worth of lignite," Frank said.

"So they say. Maybe we should be prospectors or wildcatters instead of ballplayers."

On Saturday morning Frank discovered that Duke had greatly exaggerated the appearance and worthiness of the Gimpy Goose, the Bisons' means of transportation. It was really a used Trailblazer bus painted red, with the big head of a bison splashed on each side. It had been equipped with a small washroom and a refrigerator, and even a small TV set. It left Grand Forks at the stroke of nine, with Devil's Lake scheduled as the first rest stop. In the seat next to Duke, Frank read that morning's *Grand Forks Record*.

"Although it is too early to make a correct appraisal of the Bisons' new look," the sports editor had written, "this writer believes that Veck's club is vastly improved. Frank Hyatt, the new second baseman, has tightened up the first line of defense and seems like a consistent hitter even though he may seldom reach the fences. Red Quinn, the bonus pitcher, looks to be just what the doctor ordered, and Guy Bondi, who starred in American Legion ball last year, has brought another long ball to the batting order. In the outfield . . ."

Duke had not exaggerated as far as the picture passing by the bus window was concerned. The flat land rolled away, acre upon acre, and it wasn't hard for Frank to imagine that the Gimpy Goose might get ambushed by a band of marauding redskins. Two hours out of Devil's Lake he got heavy-eyed, tossed a pocked-sized whodunit aside and fell asleep.

———————

A door slammed shut and shook Frank awake, and he looked up at Danny Sloat and realized that he was in the apartment in Milwaukee again. The Chiefs' relief pitcher fired his plaid sports jacket toward a chair. "I should have stood in bed, too," he said. "I got hooked for an outdoor performance of *Macbeth* by a bunch of summer students at the college. "Oh, brother!" He struck a dramatic pose. " '. . . a poor player that struts and frets his hour upon the diamond—er—stage, and then is heard no more. A tale told by an idiot, full of sound and fury, signifying nothing.' You know something, Frank? That could be a soliloquy on a broken-down ballplayer."

"It certainly could." He got up from the easy chair still hearing the singing of bus tires, feeling the vibration of the Gimpy Goose. He looked out of the window, half expecting to see cattle grazing as far as the eye could reach, and farmers plowing up a vast expanse of field.

Duke asked, "Don't you feel all right? You're sweating over the fact that you might get to play tomorrow in Duhamel's place? Isn't that what you've been waiting for?"

"Sure, Danny, like a kid waiting to get a tooth drilled for the first time. And you're as cool as a cucumber, so why are you chewing at your nails again? Won't that affect your grip on a ball?"

"You tagged me that time." The pitcher laughed, and nodded. "That Shakespeare stuff bugged me, Frank. I should have insisted on a Bob Hope movie." He dropped down on the bed. "I have been up before. Front office brass, as well as players, are superstitious, and how often do they take a pitcher to the well?"

"Get the cards out, Danny. Some gin rummy will get it off our minds."

"Will it be a hundred or a thousand dollars a point?"

Out over a million an hour later, Danny Sloat said he would pay Frank when he got control of the New York Bomber club, and got ready for bed. Frank turned in about the same time, but sleep was slow in coming. When his roomie began to snore, his mind strayed once more and picked up the Gimpy Goose when it got to Rugby, a little town about eighty miles from Minot.

―――――――――――

The Bisons, after taking the series from the Nesters, roared though their first thirty games with only nine losses and Frank wrote Tom Thorp that the bat he had sent him just after the first visit to Minot had to be full of magic, for most of the balls that were bouncing off it had

47

eyes. He was hitting .289, the highest average he'd ever reached. Beginning with three games under the lights at Aberdeen, however, Mike Kaska, the leading RBI man, dropped into a woeful slump, and all the known good luck charms, along with Mike's and the manager's corrective measures, failed to work. The Grand Forks club slipped from second place to fourth in less than two weeks.

Opening a series with Fargo at home, Frank got a double to the left field corner his first time at bat, and pulling up at the middle station he hoped that something Veck had said just before the game was not just a rumor. The Austin Colts in Class AA were in trouble, and a Milwaukee scout was combing the bushes for talent. He had been seen at the hotel earlier in the day. There was a possibility that he would take a long look at a man hitting .291.

He died on second when the Blue Sox pitcher got Vance, Tannone, and his mound rival, Bob Hightower, out in order. The Bison southpaw returned the compliment in the top of the third, and the crowd yelled for the home club to get some runs when Duke Lubell went out to lead off. Duke grounded out to third, but both Monnegan and Guy Bondi singled, leaving it up to big Mike Kaska. The fans were on the slugger. They yelled for a pinch hitter, and Kaska turned away from the plate and walked back to the dugout. "How about it, Frank?" he asked. "Let me use your hot bat."

He looked at Kaska as if the man had gone out of his mind. "Not in a million years, Mike," he said.

Veck yelled, "Why not, Hyatt? Are you playing just for yourself, or for the interests of the rest of the team?"

The ump ordered the manager to get a batter to the plate and Veck shouted, "Hold your horses, Bill. Give

48

me a couple more seconds." Then he swung back toward Frank, a certain look in his pale blue eyes. It said that the second baseman was with the Bisons mostly on his say-so alone, that he owed Veck something.

The quiet along the bench added to the pressure put upon him. He nodded, and said in a small, tight voice, "Okay, Mike." He felt as if the slugger were carrying no less than one of his arms out to the plate.

Kaska leaned back from the first pitch, and then swung and missed at a sweeping curve. He got two more bad pitches, then looked up the line at the man directing traffic at third. The green light flashed for him and he swung from his heels at the three and one delivery. The heavy end of the bat, broken clean off, spun toward the pitcher's mound, and the ball blooped out into right field for a single, and Monnegan raced around third to score. Mose Valentine, before he stepped in to take his cut, picked up the handle of the bat and fired it toward the Bison bench. Duke Lubell made himself heard above the crowd's noise. "Frank, you sucker! Oh, you're a nice guy!"

He felt a sickness inside him that left little room for anger. The blame he directed mostly toward himself. Veck put a hand on his shoulder, "It was a sacrifice in a way, kid, and maybe it'll pay off. That hit could get Mike back in the groove again. After all, a bat is a bat, Frank, not a magic wand."

"If you say so," Frank snapped, and went to the on-deck circle with a bat he'd never hefted before. Up to this point it seemed to him that to get something you had to give up too much in return. His head snapped up when Mose slammed a hit off the Blue Sox first baseman's glove, bringing Bondi in with the second run for Grand Forks. The crowd gave him a big round of applause when he dug himself in at the plate. They pleaded with him to keep the rally alive.

His confidence oozed out of him with his sweat, and after running the count one and two, he drove the ball to short to give the Blue Sox the easy double play.

He went nothing for four that night, and the Sox beat Hightower with a long ball in the first of the ninth, 6-4. Kaska had hit two singles and a long triple. In the dressing room he put a big hand on Frank's shoulder. "I'm sorry, kid. I'm going to get you a new bat, tailor-made by a guy who sells them to big leaguers like Willie Mays and Harmon Killibrew. You just give me your height and weight, the length of your arms and——"

"Forget it, Mike."

He hurried into his street clothes, and soon he and Duke were on their way to their trailer home. The shortstop, ignoring a stop light, said, "I'll tell you what I'd have done. I would have wrapped another bat around Kaska's fat neck!"

"You didn't think it wasn't in my mind, Duke?"

"Someday maybe you'll obey an impulse," the shortstop ground out. "This is just boot camp, where you develop an image that will be written down in a book. When you get to the real wars they'll judge you by it. You've got just two cheeks on your face, Frank. What do you do after they've belted them both out of shape?"

"Duke, I owe Veck a lot. He——"

"You owe nothing to nobody but yourself. If you'd flopped at that training camp you would have been told to hit the road and they wouldn't have asked did you have bus fare or enough money for one square meal."

Frank stared straight ahead. Maybe Duke was a hundred per cent right, but he directed his mind to think otherwise.

FIVE

DURING THE NEXT TWO WEEKS FRANK HYATT'S BATTING average dropped nearly thirty points and he was dropped to eighth position in the Bison batting order, and only the fact that the rest of the club was hitting, he was sure, kept him off the bench. After a bad night in Pierre, South Dakota, Veck took him aside. "You're a victim of a fixation, not the pitchers, Frank. Tom Thorp gave you a bat and he has Indian blood in him, but I never knew he was a medicine man. And you've been swinging hard, something you never used to do. Make up your mind that beginning tomorrow night you'll just try to meet the ball."

He got a scratch hit out of four tries in the get-away game, and his batting average was .246 when the Bisons boarded the bus for the long long trip home. He hoped a letter would be waiting for him there.

Tom Thorp had not disappointed him. "After reading your letter a couple of times," the ex-ballplayer had written, "I think your main trouble is that you're feeling sorry for yourself. I'd be glad to send you a bat just like that other one, and for free, but I'm not going along with that crazy idea of yours that any club I send you is blessed by the Great Spirit. Instead, I'm giving you some advice, some you must have forgotten that I gave you once before. When you face a pitcher, you keep that left elbow sticking out and sight the ball over it as the pitch comes in."

Frank read the rest of the letter, mostly concerned with news of his home town, and very little of it registered. He crammed it back into its envelope and had to admit he'd been grasping at a false religion involving omens, charms and signs, and had neglected to believe in himself.

"Who do you think the Scots will send against us Monday night, Duke?" he asked.

"Most likely the left-hander, Roy Banneman. He's beaten us three times."

They had been on the road for nearly nine hours and were travel-weary, and even though it was Saturday night they put the lights out at ten o'clock. After a late breakfast the next day, Frank made his way to a nearby trailer and rapped on the door. It was occupied by a North Dakota student and his wife. Curt Nielson was the college's ace hurler, a tall and husky man with a blond crew cut. "No, we don't want to borrow any eggs, Curt," Frank said when the big man swung the door open. "I thought maybe we could go out there in the field and you could pitch a few. I guess you know what I'm hitting."

"Sure, Frank," Nielson said. "I'll be right with you."

A few minutes later, the Bison second baseman, keep-

52

ing Thorp's suggestion in mind, swung at the college hurler's assortment of pitches. He sensed an immediate improvement when he started hitting a few solid drives, but Nielson had some criticism of his own. "Frank, you're doing something a little wrong. Our coach straightened out a couple of our guys along the same line. You don't mind a Joe College giving you advice?"

Frank laughed. "Curt, right now I'd listen to tips from a Girl Scout."

"The swing of the bat has to be level, parallel to the ground, and any upward or downward movements of your wrist from a level position will cause you to miss or hit a pop fly. Or top the ball. I've noticed you doing that."

The second baseman shook his head slowly from side to side. "You know I'd forgotten that, Curt? Left it all back somewhere. Thanks for the help."

The college pitcher threw some more pitches and Frank started hanging out clotheslines toward the apple trees a hundred yards away. Nielson finally called a halt. "I put some good stuff on those pitches, Frank. Sorry, I have to go. I must take the old lady to church." He grinned. "Tell the Bisons I'll send them a bill."

"Not until after you see what I do against the Scots tomorrow night," Frank said, laughing.

The Bisons, a few percentage points out of second place, drew a sizable crowd. The harmonica trio was there, and hundreds of the distaff side had been let in for half price. They were making a lot of noise while the Bisons took infield practice. Lubell yelled over to Frank from short, "The shrieker sex! No squirting tobacco juice tonight."

Near game time news reached the Grand Forks bench that brought wide grins and sighs of relief. Banneman, after warming up, had felt a stiffness in his shoulder and would not start. A little righthander started throwing, and Guy Bondi said, "It looks like Salvada, the guy they just brought up from semi-pro ball in Sioux Falls. Man, he burns them in."

Kaska laughed. "I was talking with the Scots' shortstop outside the hotel this morning. The kid lost four pounds on his first road trip. All he knew how to order in English was ham and eggs and he had them three times every day until the other guys finally set him straight."

"I hope he flops trying to locate the plate here," Duke said, and got up. "Well, it's just about that time." Veck hustled the team out to the diamond, and the welcome-back roar chased after them. After the national anthem, Van Lingle rubbed up a new ball, then dug a toe hold for himself on the mound. Boos showered the first man to come away from the visitors' bench with a bat.

It was a hot night. Myriad insects swarmed over the light towers, and the infielders' spikes barely bit into the sun-baked skin of the diamond. Frank knew both sides would be fighting the bad hops. Duke Lubell was the first victim when the Scot leading off drove Lingle's pitch to short. Duke had to leap to get the high bounce and by the time he threw to Kaska, the runner was across the bag. Lingle got ahead of the next hitter, then resorted to the screwball he hoped might get him to faster company some day, and struck his man out. Working on the murderous part of the Scots' batting order, he made two attempts to pick the base runner off. They called Joey Jankowitz the Flying Scot, for he had a record thus far of eighteen stolen bases.

The count on the hitter, two and two, Guy Bondi called for a pitchout, and his hunch was right, for Jankowitz streaked for second. Frank took the throw that was in the dirt and he was lucky to stop the ball from going out into center. The Aberdeen cleanup man singled the runner home, but was out a few moments later on the front end of a double play, Tannone to Hyatt to Kaska.

Both pitchers started off as hot as the night, and at the end of two and a half innings neither side had come up with anything that resembled a hit. Salvada struck out George Vance, the Bison right fielder, leading off in the last of the third, and when Frank left the on-deck station, one of the harmonica players turned loose a sour note. The fans booed. He cocked his bat close to his right ear, kept that left elbow out and held his head still. His eyes followed Salvada's first pitch from the moment the man had started his delivery, and he drove it to the opposite field for a clean single.

Lingle bunted foul on a third strike and was out, but Duke Lubell got a handle-hit over short, and the fans came fully alive. They turned quiet and abusive once more when Lew Monnegan popped up to the Scot catcher, and only a small few yelled encouragement out to Guy Bondi, who was hitting next. The big catcher took a ball, then two strikes. Salvada reared back and fired his blazer, and Bondi hit it far over the right field fence.

The Bisons got Salvada out of there in the fifth after Frank had driven in two runs with a double down the right field line and went on to pound two relief pitchers for sixteen hits and a 12-4 win. In the dressing room after his shower, Frank felt like a man who had been freed of handcuffs. He grinned from ear to ear when Mike Kaska said, as he walked past, "Hello, Slugger!" He was sure glad Ben wasn't around, for he would be a soft touch at this moment.

55

As the pennant race unwound in the Dakotas he grad-ually raised his batting average to its proper level, .268, and Veck put him back into the sixth spot in the batting order. The Bisons were hard on the heels of the league-leading Pierre Saints with less than three weeks to go. The night they were to open a two-game set with the Fargo Blue Sox, Veck dropped the word that Harry Frye, in charge of the Milwaukee farm system, along with one of the Chief scouts, was making the rounds of the far-away places, taking an estimate of the young talent.

"Sure," Duke said to Frank, as he examined the spikes on his shoes, "they'll still be looking for the muscle-men, the long ball, and a couple of hot pitchers like Lefty Grove or Walter Johnson. You can be a two-eighty or -ninety Punch and Judy hitter with a fielding average of a thousand, but——"

"Oh, I don't know, Duke. Unless you get a couple of runners on, the home runs don't mean so much. First it has to be the twang of a banjo before the boom of the big drum."

Veck started Red Quinn against Fargo. The Blue Sox countered with their southpaw, Vic Dente, and at the end of five full innings there were only goose eggs on the scoreboard. In the top of the sixth, the Blue Sox's three hundred hitter, Holliman, rocketed a pitch over the fence in center after two were out, and the one-run lead still stood up until the Bisons came in for the last of the eighth. When Frank took a bat from the rack, Veck said, "Get on, Frank, any way you can. I need this game."

He went up to hit, one for three thus far, the crowd solidly with him. Dente kept the ball low, trying to put it across the batter's knees, but his sinker would not work for him and he found himself behind, three and one. He tried to cross Frank up with a high one, fast and inside, and it grazed the batter's shirt and gave him the free ticket to first. After Dente threw a strike past Vance, Veck's first base coach called time to talk to his base runner. "Break up a possible double play. Dump the keystone man if you can."

Taking his lead off first, Frank knew neither Tannone nor Red Quinn would hit if the Bisons kept a man on. Ed Workman, an outfielder, was looking over the lumber at the Bison bench. Vance missed with two bunt attempts, and with the hit sign on, he drove a pitch on the ground between first and second. The Fargo shortstop took the quick throw from his second baseman and forced Frank, but before he could complete the double play his feet were knocked out from under him. Before the cloud of dust cleared away, Frank knew it had cost him. The pain of a twisted ankle locked his jaws and turned his sweat cold. He stayed down.

Veck and three other Bisons came out, one of them Hy Fox, a first-aid man of sorts but a much better bus driver. He took off Frank's left shoe and explored the injured ankle with fingers anything but expert. "All I'm sure of, Fred," he said to the manager, "It isn't busted. Let's get him to the bench."

A man came out of the stands and met them before they crossed the third base line. Veck shouted, "Hello, Doc. I'm sure glad you're here," and Frank forced a smile. "Not Ben Casey?"

"Just Smith," the doctor said. After a preliminary examination he said to Veck, "This should be tended to right away, Fred. If somebody will help me with him my car is out in the parking area."

"Let's go," Hy Fox said.

Just as the doctor's car left the parking area the sound of a crowd-burst came out of the ball park, and Frank, his left leg held out straight on the back seat, guessed George Vance, the man he had kept alive, was running the bases. But his thoughts turned dismal. What he had been ordered to do was part of the game, and it involved a calculated risk, but why did it always seem to be Frank Hyatt who was expendable in one way or another?

Twenty minutes later, in his office, Doc Smith said, "A bad sprain, Frank. You won't be playing ball for the rest of this summer." He applied a firm bandage over the joint to limit internal bleeding, then went to a closet and brought out a pair of crutches. "Rest all you can. The bandage should be removed once or twice a day and the ankle treated with hot or cold applications."

"I guess I don't live right," Frank said huskily, "or would it be too right?"

"I'll think that over when I get time," the doctor said. "Well, let's get going."

Duke arrived at the trailer a few minutes after the doctor had driven off. "We won it in eleven innings, 3-1. Workman tripled Vance in to tie it, and—how's the ankle, Frank? How long——?"

"I have to wait until next year." He lay back on the bed and closed his eyes and felt like bawling. "Y-You play good tomorrow night, Duke. You get up to even Class AAA maybe, and you'll tell them about the other half of that best double-play combo in the minors."

"Yeah." Duke peeled off and got into his pajamas, whistling a famous TV singer's theme song, "Dream along with me-e-e-e-e, I'm on my way-y-y-y to the stars!" . . . "Frank, they're not going to dump you for getting hurt. So you miss the last few games——"

"Out of sight, out of mind, Duke. My absence won't make their hard hearts grow fonder of me."

"I'm going to tell you something. I got it from Veck on

the last trip to Fargo, but you weren't supposed to know in case it put pressure on you. Harry Frye watched you play in Bismark and at Minot and he's high on you. One will get you five you'll be with the Austin Colts next year."

"Thanks for telling me, Duke. I'll give you the same odds that says somebody's relative is to be moved along instead."

"Well, you won't be at Grand Forks next year, Frank. The Chiefs haven't more than a working agreement with the Bisons, and the last copy of the *Sporting Gazette* implies that they intend to withdraw that. Attendance dropped off in Milwaukee this year and the Chiefs are going to have to be careful with their wampum."

Frank stayed in Grand Forks. He had thrown his crutches away and was leaning on a cane the night the Bisons suited up to play the first game of the last series of the year with the Bismark Senators. Veck's club had to sweep the three-game set and pray that the Saints would lose their last two to Minot if they were to get a first place tie. Veck had an eighteen-year-old kid not long out of high school at second. He was hitting .201.

At the end of the fifth inning a lot of the fans kissed the pennant good-bye and began to leave their seats. The Senators had chased Red Quinn, Lingle and Vance, who had been taken out of left field and used as a fireman. They led, 9-1. Two errors by the high school player had led to five unearned runs, and when the Bisons came in from the field after holding off the visitors in the first of the seventh, Veck grinned at Frank. "You could say we lost the pennant by a sprained ankle. You know of a good job for an old man anywhere, Frank?"

He felt sorry for Veck as he watched the potent part of the Bison batting order try to make the score a little less painful. Veck lived and talked baseball, and he hadn't left much room in his mind for anything else. There would be nothing for him to do outside unless he worked with his hands.

Lew Monnegan got on and Guy Bondi hit safely behind the runner and there were men on first and third. The Senator pitcher worked too carefully on Mike Kaska and walked him, and the Bismark pilot went out to the hill and asked for the ball. Mose Valentine, enjoying a ten-game hitting streak, greeted the relief pitcher with a screaming drive into the gap between center and left, clearing the bases, and the score was 9-4. The fans left in the seats yelled for more, and George Vance responded by driving Mose in. The Senators' manager took a walk to the mound again. A few minutes later the Bison uprising was put down, and only a handful of spectators were around when the home team made their last bid in the ninth.

Early in September when they vacated the trailer, Frank left his cane behind. His ankle felt strong and he knew it had not sustained the slightest bit of damage to come back to plague him. It was hard saying good-bye to Duke. Tritely he said, "Don't take any wooden nickels. Keep in touch if——"

"Sure. They'll shuffle the minor league deck in Milwaukee this winter, deal out the honor cards and discard the rest." He laughed and shrugged his shoulders. "Are we higher than the ten-spot? I'd like to think I was a one-eyed Jack. Come on, I'll drive you to the station before we get sloppy."

"Don't look back," the shortstop said when Frank got out of the car," I want to remember you just as you are. See you around." He threw the jalopy into gear and drove off, and Frank smiled and swallowed hard as if something had stuck in his throat.

He took the train to Minneapolis, then to Chicago, and changed there for White River, but he did not quite make it.

———

His train of thought was shunted off tracks long grown over with weeds by a voice of the present, and he was back in Milwaukee again. Danny Sloat said, "I had to wake you up, Frank. You kept tossing around and mumbling in your sleep. Tell me something if it isn't too personal. Why do you want to be a one-eyed Jack?"

It took him a few moments to convince himself that he was really where he was, that he was a big league player. He gave Danny an embarrassed look and said, "You've heard of a subconscious? Mine seldom leaves me alone."

"You'd better lock it in this room tonight. We're playing the Metros at seven fifty-five," the Milwaukee relief pitcher threw at him. "The paper this morning said you'll most likely start in Duhamel's place."

"Most likely? That doesn't mean positively, does it?"

Sloat said, "You know anything that's sure in this life, Frank? Only that you never leave it alive."

"I'd like to do one thing before they call out my number, Danny. Get up to bat just once in the major leagues. I've been in the on-deck circle, waiting, for almost eight years."

"And I've pitched almost eighty games in the bullpen." Sloat laughed. "We really belong together."

SIX

BALLPLAYERS EVERYWHERE, WHEN A NIGHT GAME IS
scheduled, have their big meal in the middle of the day.
Danny and Frank took a bus to downtown Milwaukee
and fortified themselves with steak, and on the way back
to the apartment Frank picked up an early edition of the
Milwaukee *Evening News* and read three sticks of boxed-
in type that shook him up. The Chiefs had brought up a
bonus player from Eau Claire, Jay Vanderpool, who was
expected to arrive in time to get into a Chief uniform that
night. He could play second, third, or short, according to
the scouts, and he had hit .288 for the Trappers.

"I like the vote of confidence they have in me," Frank
said, and tossed the paper into Danny's lap.

"Don't let it throw you," the pitcher said after he'd
read the story. "This time of year they load up with all
the young talent they can afford; and don't forget, the

Chiefs have a fair chance to grab second money. Insurance is the big kick everywhere nowadays."

"Sure." Frank grinned, "I'll tell them right out, Danny. Play me or trade me."

The Chiefs were getting into their white home uniforms a little over five hours later when the infielder from Eau Claire came into the dressing room. He was a tall and rangy sandy-haired youth wearing clothes that were all the rage on the college campuses, and Frank looked for but found not the slightest trace of unease or awe in the man's brown eyes. After all, he mused, if you give a man of tender years the sum of sixty thousand dollars to sign his name on a piece of paper, you couldn't expect an inferiority complex.

Kelso came out of the trainer's room when he got the word of the rookie's arrival, and Frank felt better when the manager refrained from spreading the verbal red carpet. He shook hands with Vanderpool, said he was glad to see him, introduced him to the other players, and told him to pick himself an empty locker. After he had suited up he was to report to his office. Frank glanced at the veterans like Joe Arriga, Ira Eckert and Hy Brown, men who hadn't saved half of sixty grand in a lifetime of baseball, and knew why they had just nodded and grunted their greetings.

Vanderpool, putting a few belongings into a locker, threw a grin down the line of half-dressed Chiefs. "I didn't expect love and kisses," he said, "and I know a lot of you resent the fact that you were born ten to fifteen years too soon. But as the old ham actor used to say, 'They loved me in Eau Claire and Peoria.' "

"We've seen the golden boys before," Al Jansky called out. "They come and go—mostly go." His laughter cleared the air. "Who said anything anyway, Vanderpool? And that name—it sounds like a lot of dough."

Duhamel came out of the Milwaukee clinic, his knee bandaged and smelling strongly of liniment. He would be in the starting lineup. "You vultures," he said good-naturedly, throwing a look at Frank, "aren't picking my bones yet."

The County Stadium was still filling when the Chiefs took the field against the last-place New York Metros, a team that after three years was beginning to jell. Dick Tomcheck, a reliever Kelso had turned into a starter, went to the mound and the crowd gave him a nice hand. Tomcheck was anything but a serious man and there were times when he delighted the fans with his histrionics. His cap always looked too small for his head, and the cuffs of his pants were practically worn at his shoe-tops.

Tomcheck breezed by the first two New York hitters and then gave up a single to the visiting right fielder. Krist, the clean-up hitter for the cellar-dwellers, ran the count to the limit, and then tripled over Raneri's head in deep center, and when Kelso appeared on the top step of the dugout his pitcher waved him back, bringing a burst of laughter from the stands. Tomcheck then proceeded to strike the fifth Metro hitter out on three pitched balls.

The Chiefs finally tied the game up in the bottom half of the fifth when Eckert hit one of McNish's fast balls out of the park, and after Tomcheck had set down the other side in order in the top of the sixth, Martsell went out to try and get something going for the Chiefs. He struck out. Richie Duhamel, after getting behind two and nothing, topped a slow roller inside the third base line, and beat the fielder's throw by a step, but pulled up lame.

Kelso swung his eyes toward Frank. "Go in and run for him, Hyatt."

The announcement of his entry into the game created very little stir in the stands. Krist, the New York first baseman, grinned at him through a big lump of tobacco as he took over the sack for Duhamel. "New man in town?" he asked, and Frank ignored him and stooped over to get two handfuls of dirt. Kelso had Tomcheck, a good hitting pitcher, bunting McNish's first pitch, and then took the sign off. Tomcheck drove a single past the incharging Metro third baseman, and Frank ran to the pickup station. Ken Provost drove him in with a long double to the right field corner, and activity stepped up in the Metro bullpen. Chiefs, 2, Metros, 1.

Frank, getting a drink at the fountain, wondered what Kelso's move would be after the third out was made. He got the answer after Johnny Drew and Joe Arriga flied out. The manager picked Vanderpool up with his eyes. "You're at second," he said.

Frank scuffed the concrete with his spikes and tried to draw Kelso's eyes his way so that the man could read the question in his own, but the manager gave the bench his broad back as he confined his attention to the field. He quickly cooled his resentment and squelched as quickly as it began a certain hope that Vanderpool would boot everything that came his way and strike out his first crack at the plate.

Out there Tomcheck quickly got into bad trouble. The Metros' number two batter singled to start the New York seventh, and the next man up drew a walk. Krist, the visitors' only three hundred hitter, stepped in. He had twenty-eight home runs. Tomcheck kept peering in at Jansky and kept shaking his head. The batter stepped out, got back in again. Again Tomcheck shook the sign off, and then Jansky went out to the mound to have a conference. The plate umpire walked halfway out there and warned against further delay of the game. Jansky left the hill, laughing and shaking his head.

"I'll bet he was telling Al one of those elephant jokes," Pete Ibarra said.

Tomcheck worked on Krist, feeding him his sinker, and after fouling off a half a dozen pitches, the slugger drove a blistering short-hopper to Vanderpool's right. The bonus rookie dug it out and fired to Provost for one. The shortstop threw to Eckert to make it two down, and the crowd applauded the play. On the bench Hy said under his breath, "A good glove." Out of the jam, Tomcheck got the next batter to pop up to Eckert.

"What was the difficulty out there, Al?" Kelso asked his catcher when the Chiefs came in for their cuts.

"I asked that jughead why he was shaking all the signs off, Sam. He said he was waiting—that maybe somebody would call Krist to the phone."

"That guy hits me good," Tomcheck said, coming away from the drinking fountain, enjoying the laugh at his expense.

Frank's attempt to join in was a weak one. He sat back and looked up at the light towers when Raneri went out to face McNish, and he had to think of Danny Sloat quoting the bard. Sure, he had reached the bright lights, but was he now the poor player who had had his hour on the stage and would be heard of no more? The fans began that rhythmic clapping of hands when Raneri singled over short. They set up a roar when Jansky hit safety to right, sending the center fielder around to third, and they pulled out all stops when Ira Eckert walked to load the bases. After Martsell struck out, Frank leaned forward on the bench and watched Vanderpool step to the plate, not a bit envious of the rookie at this moment of tension, where men were separated from the boys.

Vanderpool was a left-handed hitter, and before Mc-Nish threw a pitch, the Metro manager hurried out to the mound, figuring to go with the percentages. He called a southpaw in, and Frank wondered if Kelso would or would not stay with Vanderpool. The manager stood pat, and Pete Ibarra said, "A hit here would pay a few bucks of that bonus back."

The New York bench worked the rookie over while the relief hurler threw his seven warmup pitches; but the racket the crowd made, Frank was certain, must have washed a lot of the razzing away from the batter's ears. Finally the Metro catcher fired the ball to his second baseman, and Vanderpool dug in, his odd stance reminding the Chiefs of Stan the Man.

The New York fireman blew a fast ball by the rookie for a strike. He missed with a breaking pitch and got his change-up too high. He threw the ball in, asked for a new one, and getting it, took his time rubbing it up. When he turned his blazer loose again, Vanderpool slashed at it and hit into a fast double play, the fans letting him know in spades that he had spoiled a big inning. The Redleg catcher said to the rookie, "Forget it, kid. They'll bleed you more than that before you're through."

Frank dropped his head close to his knees. You'd better believe it, Vandy, he said to himself. I've been stabbed with so many needles for so long I should be getting transfusions.

Tomcheck fouled out to the backstop, then strode to the mound with a 3-1 lead. He walked the first hitter to face him and then gave up a single, and Frank grinned along with the other Milwaukee reserves when the pitcher stared in at the dugout as if daring Kelso to come out there and yank him. With the visor of his cap shading most of his left ear, Tomcheck bowed his neck and struck the third batter out. Pete Ibarra observed, "Sometimes I think the knucklehead does it on purpose. He likes to get into a hole and work himself out."

The veteran hurler gave the Metro third baseman a pitch that sank, and the ball was hit straight at Provost, who fired to Vanderpool covering second. The bonus kid dropped the throw, and instead of a twin killing to end the inning the sacks were jammed with Metros. Tomcheck, who had left the hill, spun around at the agonized groan from the crowd. He glanced out at Vanderpool, jettisoned some tobacco juice, then went back to work again. A pinch hitter drove in the Metro's second run with a towering sacrifice fly to Arriga, and the New York manager drew on his bench again.

"It's old Ed Nagursky," Hy Brown said, before the announcement was made. "He can still kill you."

Kelso went out in front of the dugout and moved his outfield pickets toward the left, and Hendryx, a utility man, chucked. "They'll throw Kelso out of the Birch society."

Tomcheck threw eleven pitches before Nagursky creamed his change-up to left center, where Raneri finally caught the ball with his back to the barrier. When the Chiefs came in, Vanderpool offered Tomcheck an apology, and the pitcher said, "You went to college, kid. Didn't they tell you why they put erasers on lead pencils when they gave you the diploma?"

Frank tried to keep his face straight. He could not see the humor in ribbing a sixty-thousand-dollar price tag, considering that he himself had come into baseball for little more than the price of a bag of peanuts. He was like a spare tire a man had bought only to leave it hanging in his garage when he took a long trip, and he could envision at the moment an item in the *Sporting Gazette* under the head "Player Transactions," as soon as winter bartering got under way: "Chiefs: Frank Hyatt, infielder, to minor league camp for reassignment." Still a ten-spot, Duke. Not even a one-eyed Jack.

The fans clamored for an insurance run when Tomcheck started the batting-go-round. He blooped a single into short center, and got around to third on ground-outs by Provost and Drew. A few pitches later, Raneri hit the Metro relief pitcher's first offering into the picnic area outside the limits of the stadium. When Arriga, also trying for the seats, popped up, Tomcheck picked up his glove, a wide grin on his bucolic face. "You guys have had your last turns at bat," he said as he left the dugout.

Frank thought the pitcher was a little too cocksure when Tomcheck began smoothing the dirt out on the hill. He threw eight pitches before he got the first batter out, and the next man up tagged him for a single to deep short. Provost made a great play on a ball but had no time to throw his man out. Krist, the New York power hitter in the on-deck circle swinging three bats, could be the tieing run, all the fans knew, if Tomcheck did not get by the batter at the plate. The pitcher threw four bad pitches in a row, and Kelso lost no time in leaving the dugout. When Zach Izzro came in from the bullpen, Kelso was still trying to get the ball away from Tomcheck, and the crowd was in fits.

"You'll be sorry, Sam," the veteran hurler said before he trudged to the showers. "I'm tellin' you, you just blew one."

Krist watched Izzro's breaking pitch sweep outside for a ball, and then he cut at a side-arm fast ball and fouled it back into the screen. Izzro changed up on him and got ahead, one and two, and Jansky fired a strike to Eckert and nearly caught the base runner leaning the wrong way. Izzro, taking plenty of time between pitches, built up tension, layer upon layer. He missed with a slider, and Krist prolonged the agony with a trip to the on-deck station to use the pine tar rag. Something told Frank it was going to be a long night when the slugger stepped back in.

Izzro checked the runners, then threw his fifth pitch in. The crack of Krist's bat made that long-gone sound. Martsell, in right, just turned to look, not run. The ball landed high up in the seats in that sector of the stadium, and three runs poured across the plate. Frank's thoughts had taken flight with that ball, and he was back on that train out of Grand Forks that had reached its destination years ago.

———

He took the bus out of Muncie to White River and arrived home just as the Hyatts were sitting down to supper, and he had taken only a few bites before his father guessed out loud that he had had enough of baseball. "You lost some weight, Frank, and I made Thorp admit the other day they did not feed you too good in the bush league. Now you've had a taste of it I figure you'll get a man's job and settle down."

"Only until next March," Frank said. "I've only had a sample, like this first helping of roast pork and gravy." He grinned at his mother and handed her his plate. "How's Ben making out?"

"He's getting along fine," Matt Hyatt said, but Frank was certain his voice lacked conviction. "He's got a man working for him who doesn't earn half the pay he gets, and no doubt has been dipping his fingers in the till. I've had it in mind for the past few weeks that it would be better to keep what money comes in from that gas station in the family. Together, you and Ben——"

"Please, not now," Frank pleaded, but his father kept pressing.

"Jobs aren't plentiful around these parts, Frank, and they don't hire a man at the plants just for a few months. You think it over."

He resisted the great temptation to tell his folks that Ben had already given him a part of the well-known business, that his big brother had blown him right out of the Little League those times with his sour trumpet. "Sure, it won't hurt to think about it," he said. The first thing he was going to do tomorrow, however, was look up Tom Thorp and get his mind clear as to the intricate workings of the big league farm system, and try to find out if a Class A ballplayer had any kind of a status at all.

When he got to his old room he discovered that it had been freshly papered, and his picture gallery removed, even the big photograph of Lou Gehrig saying good-bye to baseball in the Yankee Stadium. He looked in the closet and rummaged through the dresser drawers but could not find them. His blood was beginning to boil a little when he heard Ben's voice below. He delayed his unpacking and hurried downstairs, to find Ben seated at the kitchen table. "Well, how's the poor man's Nellie Fox?" his brother asked, his sense of humor as warped as ever.

Frank forced a smile and asked, "And how's the new lunch counter doing?"

Ben's grin quickly fell from his face. "Look, Frank," he said, "the highway isn't coming through here, so I put in a lot of stock like tires, batteries and——" He glanced at his folks, the old appeal in his eyes, and they did not disappoint him.

Matt Hyatt said to Frank, "You'd better understand something right now. I'll have no more of the old bickering."

"There needn't be any problem here," Frank said. "I'm sure I can rent a room from Mrs. Thorp. And somebody tell me what happened to the pictures I had on the wall up there."

Ben said, keeping his eye on the plate he had just wiped clean of gravy with a piece of bread, said, "We figured you was through with that kid stuff so we—you'll find 'em in the cellar, Frank."

"I'll be finished with them when this country gives up baseball!"

● SEVEN

HE SLEPT UNTIL NINE O'CLOCK THE NEXT MORNING, AND after assuring his mother at breakfast that he had dismissed a break with his family out of his mind, went down into town to Tom Thorp's auto repair shop. When he walked in, Tom was just crawling out from under a Chevvy. "Well, well," Thorp said, and jumped to his feet. He banged a fist against a fender. "The trouble was in the clutch, where I most generally had it, myself. I'll shake hands after I wash up."

When they were in the cluttered little office, Thorp eyed his protégé for a few moments while he stuffed an old briar with tobacco. "I got a report on you from Fred Veck a couple of weeks ago, Frank. 'A good everyday player and a consistent spray hitter, and has an adequate glove. Nothing sensational.' But don't let that discourage you, for seventy per cent of major league players come under that category. The big stars would be nothing without supporting casts."

"But what next, Tom, if Grand Forks folds completely? Do I make the rounds of the training camps next year with a bag in my hand and——?"

"That's a good baseball town. If Milwaukee dumps it some other major league club will take it over, I'm sure. After all, it only had a working agreement with the Chiefs. Despite all this paying of big bonus money to high shool and college stars, the minors are where the big leagues develop ninety per cent of their players. And an awful lot of 'em jump right from Double A to the big show. Yes, even from Class A. You stop worrying and keep yourself in shape during the winter. I advise you to get a job that keeps you out of doors a lot—one that involves plenty of physical exercise." He stabbed the stem of his pipe at Frank. "Two things I know when I start dissecting them—an auto engine and a ballplayer."

"I sure hope you're always right." Frank got up when we saw a tow truck bring a car into the yard. "I see you're going to be pretty busy, Tom, so I'll see you later."

"Drop over at the house the first chance you get."

He hopped a bus to Ben's Filling Station on the outskirts of the town and it occurred to him that his brother might well have spent some of the money he'd loaned him for some cans of paint. There were three cars at the pumps getting serviced, the hired man doing most of the work while Ben, with his head stuck inside one of the cars, talked to the man at the wheel. A few moments later he followed Ben into his little office and said, "Like I told Dad, I've thought it over. I'll throw in with you and see how it works."

Ben held out his hand. "It's a deal, Frank. Shake on it."

"There's conditions, Ben. No bosses. We split two ways."

Before he left he checked Ben's books and found that too many local citizens had been put on the cuff for services rendered. "The first thing I do is collect on these," he said. Then he suggested that his brother let the hired help know right away that he was through at the end of the week.

"Frank, I wanted to talk about that," Ben said, keeping his eyes everywhere but on his brother. "I guess you know I haven't had a vacation for a long time, and now that you're here—well, I figured I could go hunting up in Michigan with Ray Caswell and Harry Lowden. Only be for two or three weeks. Frank, I do need a rest." He put on that front that had paid off for years, and for good measure he said he hadn't been feeling well for some time.

"Sure, Ben. I guess it'll be all right. I'll be ready to take over here on Monday morning." When he rode back to town he felt like a yokel who had been relieved of both his gold watch and his wallet at a country fair, or like a base runner who had fallen for the ancient hidden-ball trick. Brothers under the skin, he said to himself. Ben had been under his skin as far back as he could remember.

Ben had his three weeks in the wilds of Michigan, but it immediately became apparent after his return that he and hard work were not exactly compatible. Frank assumed the lion's share of the burden, and when autumn turned to winter it was as plain as an umpire's call that he would be very lucky to get forty per cent of the net proceeds, to say nothing of the slightest return on that five-hundred-dollar loan. There was a fringe benefit, though—a gain of nearly six pounds of hard flesh that just might help propel a baseball off a bat another fifty feet. As Tom Thorp reminded him, there was a bright side to everything, even working for Ben.

In early January the hot stove league began sizzling, and ballplayers in the higher brackets winced at the whine of the winter trade winds and shuddered at the possibility of salary cuts. Minor leaguers, particularly, sweated out reassignments and outright releases. Even before the old year had faded out, Frank had read in the *Sports Gazette* that Grand Forks had been dropped from the Milwaukee chain. Early in February he got the notification that he had been reassigned to the Class A Boise club in the Rocky Mountain Loop.

He took his discouragement to Tom Thorp, and that man overhauled him as if he had been a sick automobile engine. "How did you get the impression you was something special, Frank? Better than a lot of Big League players up there today, most of whom spent as much as five years in the minors? They had the guts and the aggressiveness to hang on. Admit it, Frank. Ben and your father have been working on your good nature again and have nearly convinced you that you'll never make as much playing ball as you could pumping gas and cleaning windshields. Do something for me just once, Frank. Put a little armor around that tender heart of yours. Assert yourself once in a while—and I don't mean that you should do it pugnaciously. Nobody's going to worry about your future but yourself."

"I'll try to remember, Tom."

He received a letter from Duke Lubell a few days later telling him that the former Grand Forks shortstop had had it. They'd shifted him to Davenport, but he was not having any. "I've had enough aggravation, indigestion and frustration to last me a lifetime, Frank," he wrote,

76

"so I'm going to bury my glove and spiked shoes and go forth to see how the other half of the world lives. I'll be rooting for you to make it all the way."

Frank packed his bags again in March. He played with Boise for two years, hitting .269 the second year and driving in fifty-nine runs as the number six hitter in the lineup. The Milwaukee club elevated him to Austin in the Double A Texas League, and there he began to see some light in the wilderness for the first time. There he played under an old Chicago Bruin outfielder, Cass Rettinger, and met Eddie Mutino and the Sanchez brothers, Pedro and Pablo, a pair of Latins he would never forget. The playing fields had better grooming; the crowds were larger, the buses longer and smoother-riding; and the food on the road no longer packed the threat of ptomaine.

In July of that year the Colts were making a bid for the pennant for the first time in five years, and Frank was hitting over .270. The infield of Pedro Sanchez at third, Eddie Mutino at short, Frank at second, and Hog Wilding at first were leading the rest of the league in double plays. The outfield, Kornauer, Pablo Sanchez and Penovi, had a combined batting average of .293. Milwaukee scouts, even at this early stage in the race, were taking good, long looks.

It had been obvious to Frank from the first of the season that Eddie Mutino was more than just in the good graces of Cass Rettinger. Eddie was twenty-six years old and whippet-lean, tipping the scales at about 170 pounds. He had close-cropped dark hair and clear hazel eyes and always seemed looking for the chance to laugh or smile. He played ball with a deadly seriousness, however, and seemed to require more time than most men after a game to restore his energy, and would almost always sit in front of his locker for fully five minutes before taking a shower. He was never without his pouch of scrap tobacco.

Rettinger's partiality toward Eddie evoked not one shred of resentment among the rest of the Colts. They just wondered, sometimes, for the manager would not even come close if he ever had the temerity to enter a popularity contest. Often, when a piece of strategy backfired, he would berate himself in the dugout, and call himself down while facing a mirror in the dressing room.

A suspicion never entered Frank's mind as the team traveled to Albuquerque in mid-July that another combination of circumstances was going to ambush him before the season was over. Everything at the moment was all right with his world, inside and outside of the ball parks. Ben had finally married and was off his financial back, and his mother had written that big brother was having his nose pushed close to the grindstone.

The Colts were a noisy and frisky bunch, particularly Hog Wilding and the Sanchez brothers. Pablo and Pedro had a mixture of English and Spanish that was rapidly giving Rettinger an ulcer and adding to the gray hairs on his head.

"What you bet, amigos," Pedro asked those in the seats around him, "that we don't get that *lanzador*, Jose Trask, in first game at Albuquerque? He is one *serpentinero* I can't heet! An' last time he gave us *dar blanqueada*, si?"

"Why don't you learn to say 'shutout,' you el knucklehead?" Hog fired back at the third baseman, and Pablo immediately backed up his brother. "You have *boca grande*, big mouth, Hog. Ees no wonder you raise *el puercos*. Ha-a-a!"

"Those razorbacks I got down on the farm learn English faster than you," Hog counterpunched. "Tell me, Pablo, what did you say to that ump yesterday that made him throw you out of the game?"

"I say not one word, no. Eet was what I said to him the day before, Hog. He looked up the words in dictionary—and so I get it the old ho-heave, si, one day later."

Following the course of the Rio Grande north, they came into a storm area, and gusts of wind shouldered along the sides of the big bus. When rain pelted down, the window next to Eddie Mutino would only come down so far, and Rettinger came from up front and suggested that the shortstop get his summer jacket on. Frank swapped glances with southpaw pitcher Mort Weiser, for the manager sounded like a father talking to a son. "Sure, Cass," Eddie said with a smile that was almost wistful, "anything you say."

It was only a two-hour ride from El Paso to Albuquerque. Thirty miles out, Hog said, "It's sure a great place for guys to come and cure insomnia. I've been counting sheep since we left Contreras. Don't they raise any pork out here?"

"The Indians," Pablo Sanchez said, "they are kosher tribes, Hog."

At noon they checked into a motel on the southeastern perimeter of the city. Frank, who roomed with Art Penovi and catcher Johnny Hagerman on the road, mentioned that certain incident of the short haul from El Paso. "Cass has just taken a shine to the guy," Penovi said, "and most likely he wants to look upon Eddie as the son he never had."

"Sure," Hagerman added. "Didn't you ever meet somebody that brought out the protective instinct in you,

Frank? And there's that something called body chemistry that just draws two personalities together, like—well, whatever is in ham and eggs or liver and bacon."

Penovi laughed. "Frank, you know now why they call a catcher's equipment the tools of ignorance. They sure fit Johnny."

An hour later they joined the Sanchez brothers, Hog Wilding and Eddie Mutino at the restaurant. Frank felt like having the minute steak that was on the menu, the price being right, but the waitress said she was sorry but they were out of steak. "Well, all right," the second baseman said, "I'll take the special."

Hog suddenly took over. "Now, just one dawg-gone minute, sister," he said, and stabbed a forefinger at a group of customers filling a long table close by. "That ain't just ham hocks they're eatin'. If this place wants the Colts' business and the patronage of all other ball clubs coming to this town, you bring Frank a steak. And bring the manager."

"Now, Hog . . ." Frank said, and the big first baseman waved him off.

Hog said, "They like to save certain dishes for the local trade, Frank. Boy, they'll push you around in this cockeyed world if you let 'em. You have to assert your-self or"—he looked up at the blond waitress—"well, what'll it be, honey?"

Frank had his minute steak, as did Art Penovi and Hagerman. When he got a look at the thin chicken sand-wich Eddie Mutino had ordered he had to ask the short-stop why. "Eddie, that isn't going to hold you up for long," he said, "and you can't eat heavy before the game tonight. If you're short of cash, I——"

"Thanks, Frank, but it's all I really want," Eddie said.

It was going to be a hot night, Frank knew, and during the course of a nine-inning ball game a man could easily sweat off a few pounds. Only good, substantial food could get that weight back on, and he wondered if Cass Rettinger shouldn't be tipped off regarding Eddie's eating habits. By the time he had finished his meal, however, he figured the best thing to do was mind his own business. Watching Pablo Sanchez finish off a plate of enchiladas, he grinned and said, "You should begin one hot hitting streak tonight, amigo."

Pedro laughed along with his brother. "Is very fonny, Frank."

That night, under the lights, the Colts kicked up their heels in the top of the first inning against the Albuquerque Pueblos. Pedro Sanchez lined out, but Penovi and Hagerman singled back to back. Pablo Sanchez doubled to left, scoring Penovi, and Hog Wilding, on a three and two count, hit one out of the park to hang up four big runs on the scoreboard.

Tod Billip, Rettinger's right-hander, made the score stand up until the last of the sixth, when with one out and a base runner on first he made the Pueblo catcher hit his pitch, a sinker that was driven just to Frank's right. He flagged it down and fired to Eddie Mutino, who failed to touch the middle sack, and Eddie's hurried throw to first was in the dirt. The ball skipped by Hog Wilding, and instead of a double play there were two runners in scoring position. Frank glanced over at Eddie, who stood there with his head bent against the crowd's hooting. When he lifted it he bent it far back and breathed in deep. The oil-shine of sweat on his face glistened in the artificial light, and his uniform looked as if he had just taken a shower and had forgotten to take it off.

The next batter for the Pueblos nailed a change-up to center to score both runners, but Billip bore down and got the side out without further damage. Frank trotted toward the dugout alongside Eddie. "That was a real rock," the shortstop said. "Guess the heat got me for a few seconds, Frank."

"We all make 'em, Eddie." His glance picked up Rettinger and he saw that the manager's attention was fixed on his shortstop. Rettinger took Eddie by the arm and walked him toward the water cooler.

"Let us go!" Pablo Sanchez chattered. "We get that launcher out in hurry an' fill the *almohadillas,* and then I get me the *jonron,* an' game ees over."

"Translate that, somebody," Hog blurted out.

"You fill the sacks," Penovi said, laughing, and he'll hit it all the way for a home run."

Pedro Sanchez was starting the batting order's third go-around. He took a bat from the rack and Pablo hopped off the bench. "Hold eet, *hermano.* That is my *madero,* an' you are not hombre enough—big enough *lenadero*— to swing it."

"Little brother wants to swing big brother's bat," Penovi explained, while Hog dropped his head in his hands and groaned. "Big brother says Pedro is not woodsman enough to swing it."

The plate umpire strode toward the dugout and angrily ordered Rettinger to get a hitter in there. Pedro, carrying his own *madero,* walked to the plate, and Penovi took over in the on-deck circle. Frank let his mind stay with Eddie Mutino. The shortstop was wiping the sweat off his face and arms with a towel. He had gotten rid of his chew of tobacco. Maybe, Frank thought, Eddie had swallowed it when he'd messed up the twin killing, and his stomach had rebelled.

Pedro Sanchez, crowding the plate, had the third pitch bounce off his shoulder and he strolled to first. Penovi singled, and the Colts were off and running again.

EIGHT

THE BUNT SIGN WAS ON FOR JOHNNY HAGERMAN, AND after working the count to two balls and a strike, he dumped a pitch too hard toward the mound. The Pueblo hurler got it on a quick hop and fired to third to force Pedro Sanchez, but the fiery Colombian made it plain to one and all that he thought otherwise as he jumped up out of a cloud of dust. "You blind like bat!" he screamed at the umpire. "I geet to pillow first, you bandido!" Pedro kicked dirt against the arbiter's trousers and was immediately ejected from the game. Rettinger stormed out of the Colts' dugout, and Pablo Sanchez, who had gone up to hit, ran up the third base line still carrying a bat.

It required the combined efforts of the Austin pilot, Pablo, and the Colt coaching at third to contain Pedro and get him off the field, while over five thousand fans howled with delight. Before he made himself invisible, the peppery infielder threw one parting shot at the man in blue. "You buy yourself eye-seein' *perro!* Which ees dog?"

Pablo Sanchez, the dust cleared away, went to the plate and tripled to deep right, scoring Penovi and Hagerman, and the Albuquerque pilot hurried out to make a pitching change. The relief pitcher got Hog Wilding to ground out between first and second, but Pablo came in with the Colts' seventh run on the put-out. Frank went to the on-deck station while Kornauer, Rettinger's center fielder, batted, but he threw his hard hat away when Kornauer struck out.

The hostile shirt-sleeved crowd clamored for a rally when the first man to face Tod Billip dropped a single into short left. The Pueblo left fielder, a .287 hitter, after getting ahead three and one, drove a hard shot to Eddie Mutino's left, and Frank lost no time getting over to take the shortstop's throw. Eddie, however, failed to come up with the ball and it went out into left center for a single, the Pueblo front runner wheeling around to third. Frank, one foot still glued to the middle sack, stared at Eddie for a long moment, then slowly went back to his position. Up to now a play like that one had been routine for the shortstop. He ran in to talk to Billip, and Hog Wilding came over from first. Rettinger, when he saw his pitcher snap at Hog and kick dirt up from the hill, lost no time getting out there. "I forgot to bring you a towel to cry in, Billip," he said, throwing a glance toward short. "All year that kid's been savin' ball games for you, and don't forget it. You can take a shower now if you don't think you've got the guts to finish."

"Look, Cass," the pitcher snapped, "What gave you the idea I'm blaming anybody? And if they get more than a run this inning I'll buy your chawing tobacco for the next thirty days!"

"It's a deal," the manager growled, and left the mound.

One of the Pueblos' heavy lumbermen flied out to shallow left, and Pablo Sanchez ran in, caught the ball and fired a strike in to Hagerman, the Albuquerque runner on third holding. Billip looked in at the Colt bench, grinned through his sweat, and then struck the next hitter out. The cleanup hitter for the Pueblos got the green light on a three and one pitch and drove it deep to left, where Pablo Sanchez hauled it in after a long run.

"All right," Rettinger said to Billip, when the pitcher came to the bench, "I was wrong. Blame it on the heat." He swung toward Eddie Mutino. "Call it quits for tonight, kid. Get your shower."

"Cass, I'm okay," the shortstop said, more than a trace of an edge to his voice, and got a bat from the rack. He turned and grinned at the manager. "Of course if that's a direct order——"

Frank, on his way out to the plate to lead off, did not catch Rettinger's reply, but at the plate, after taking a breaking pitch for a strike, he swung his head around and saw Eddie in the on-deck circle, swinging two bats over his head.

He took another fast ball that hummed just above his knees and got behind, but the third pitch was just the kind he liked and he punched it into short right for a single. He had a good lead off first when Eddie topped a slow roller between first and the mound and he got to the pick-up station without drawing a throw, and threw his glance toward first when Eddie was out by two steps. It was the kind of leg-hit the shortstop had always beaten out nineteen times out of twenty, and Frank involuntarily shook his head as he watched Eddie return to the bench at a half-trot.

Billip waved his bat at three pitches as gracefully as most hurlers, and Tony Acerbo, filling Pedro Sanchez's shoes, popped out to the Albuquerque catcher.

The first batter for the home club in the bottom of the inning hit to deep short, Eddie digging it out close to the outfield turf. He straightened, fired across the diamond to Hog, way short, but the first baseman stretched himself to the limit and scooped it up for the put-out. Cass Rettinger came off the visitors' bench and called time, strolled out to the coaching box at third and waved Eddie Mutino in. After a short conference, Rettinger slapped Eddie on the back and took him in tow. Bernie Jewell, utility infielder-coach, trotted out to the shortstop position. Hog Wilding yelled at Eddie above the steady racket from the stands, "Maybe next time you'll eat that steak!"

The Pueblos failed to get a thing going against Tod Billip for the rest of the hot night, and the Colts galloped off with a 7-2 win. When they filled the dressing room, they found Pedro Sanchez stretched out on the long bench, a transistor radio balanced on his bare midriff and blaring way-out music. Pedro seemed fully detached from it all until his brother Pablo poured half a can of Coke over his swarthy face. "You one el fakir!" he said, "Ees one way you get out of hot night, si? If I am the managero, I would fine you mucho dinero."

"I still say eet. I was robbed!" Pedro shouted. He sat up and turned the radio off. "What happened to Eddie? He say not one word to Pedro, jus' took the shower and walk out."

"Something he ate, I guess," Penovi said, and peeled off his sweat-soaked flannel shirt. "I'll bet it was over a hundred out there tonight."

"Ees hot, amigo?" Pablo laughed. "You should play in

Caribbean League. Down there when dog chases the cat they both walk."

Frank, dressing alongside Hagerman, mentioned to the catcher that they should look in on Eddie when they returned to the motel, and Rettinger overheard. "Just let him alone," he advised, stepping in closer. "Let him rest."

Reveling in the air-conditioned unit half an hour later, Frank said, "I wonder how it would feel to be the apple of a manager's eyes, to always get a pat on the back whether you booted one or turned in a fielding gem. Now do not get me wrong, you guys. Eddie is just about the easiest guy to like I've ever known. No envy is involved, believe me. But to know somebody close to the brass is looking after your interests must give you that old incentive."

"Frankly, I like things just as they are, as far as I am concerned," Art Penovi said. "The less I have to do with a manager the better I'll get along. Eddie? He just needs a couple of days off."

Frank stretched out on his bed and closed his eyes, wishing he could rid his mind of certain misgivings and tell himself why his thoughts often drifted back to his brother Ben whenever he was in Eddie's company. It made no sense whatsoever, for the shortstop was as different from Ben in both looks and personality as water was from rock. Rettinger's deep concern over Eddie had no reason to bother him in the slightest, yet he could not shake off the feeling that in some way and very soon he was going to become involved. He had been born that kind of guy. All at once he recalled Tom Thorp's advice and made up his mind to heed it. As sure as there would never be another Babe Ruth, the nice guys as well as the tough guys in this profession would knock the cover off a soft heart as soon as they would off a baseball if it meant climbing to a higher rung on the ladder.

Coming out of the restaurant with three other Colt players the next morning, Frank met Eddie coming in. Art Penovi said, "You get yourself a good breakfast, you hear? How do you feel?"

"Fine," the shortstop said, and Frank agreed, with reservations. There were plain signs of fatigue still clouding the shortstop's hazel eyes. "It's that business they call basic or basal metabolism," Eddie explained through a grin. "Like food I take in doesn't break down right in my cells or organisms. So sometimes I get bushed without any notice."

Pablo Sanchez nudged Frank. "So you think me an' Pedro talk so funny, si? You tell me what he said."

"I don't understand Greek either," the second baseman said.

"I'll be in there tonight," Eddie said, and left them there.

A half hour before game time that night, Eddie started jawing at Cass Rettinger when he learned his name had been omitted from the lineup. He was the best judge as to how he felt and he wasn't going to be treated like a kid that had just recovered from the chicken pox. Neither Cass nor any other guy was going to break up a good hitting streak.

The manager let him run his verbal string all the way out before making his own pitch. "You were told one time, Eddie," he said quietly, "just how far you could go."

The storm suddenly cleared from Eddie's eyes and for a moment Frank thought they became frightened. "Cass, I'm sorry," the shortstop said. "Y-You're the doctor."

"Yeah." Rettinger took a deep breath, got up from his

chair and yelled at his ball club. "What are you waiting for? Get out there and loosen up."

Long after the Pueblo pitcher had thrown his first pitch, Eddie Mutino's incipient rebellion kept plaguing Frank. It was as if Rettinger held a club over the shortstop—as if there had been a deep secret between them. Stepping out of the batter's box in the top of the fifth to get dirt on his hands, he glanced toward the Colts' bench and Eddie gave him an encouraging wave of his hand and yelled something he could not quite sift out of the noise in the stands.

There was a runner, Hog Wilding, on second and one man was out, and the Pueblos had a 3-1 lead. Frank worked the string even, two and two, then hung a clothesline into left close to the foul line for what the Sanchez brothers called a "tubey," a two-base hit. It was his second hit of the game and it upped his batting average to .270. Bernie Jewell, Eddie Mutino's immediate replacement, beat out a handle-hit, but Frank was flagged down rounding third. He scored the third run for the Colts a few moments later on pitcher Ownie Mattison's ground-out to the Pueblo second baseman. Reaching the bench he got a slap on his derriere from Rettinger, and for some reason he wished it had been a dressing down.

After Pedro Sanchez flied out to right, Frank trotted out to the inner defense, reaching back for some comforting words he had read in the *National Sports Gazette* the day before. "Colt second baseman Frank Hyatt must have a soft spot in his heart for Dudley Field in El Paso," a scribe wrote. "In the last visit there, he banged out five hits against an assortment of Sun Devil pitchers. Property of the Milwaukee Chiefs . . ."

The Albuquerque leadoff hitter slammed a hot

grounder to his right and he backhanded the ball just a foot from the keystone sack, spun around and rifled it to Hog. The runner protested to high heaven when he was called out, and the Pueblo pilot hurried out to put in his own beef. The *afficionados* in the seats howled like a wolf pack and showered the field with paper cups and seat cushions. Over at third, Pedro Sanchez waved a white handkerchief at the spectators, then stretched out flat on the ground. The pantomime cleared the air and reversed the crowd's mood.

Ownie Mattison cut two more Albuquerque hitters down and the Colts moved in again to swing some lumber. "You beeg showboater," Pablo said to his brother," one beeg hamero, si?"

"I help save blood of Señor umpire," Pedro said.

Hog Wilding guffawed. "Huh—they bleed?"

The Pueblo pitcher hobbled the Colts in the top half of the seventh, and Bernie Jewell started Mattison off badly when he allowed a hard infield grounder to skip between his legs. Alerted for the bunt, Pedro Sanchez and Hog Wilding edged in when Mattison threw to the next Pueblo batter. Pedro was halfway into the plate when the man swung from his heels and he had time only to block the wicked line drive partially with his glove. His head did the rest, and he staggered backward a few steps and then sat down hard on the seat of his pants. The fans came up screaming at one of the craziest plays they had ever seen. Ownie Mattison took the carom off Pedro's head and fired to first to get the runner by half a step.

Cass Rettinger ran out to the diamond with trainer-coach Ky Webling and shoved Colt players away from Pedro. The Latin's eyes were a little out of focus and he was saying he had never seen such glorious fireworks at any fiesta. When Pablo arrived from the outfield and took a look at the lump over his brother's left eye, he shrugged and said, "So long as it heet him in the head he is mucho okay."

"I'd say it was quite a painful assist," Hog Wilding said as Webling applied first aid. Pedro, his eyes clearing, finally grinned up at the Colt manager. After he was stood on his feet he glanced toward the man coaching for the home club at third.

"Señor, it ees all right to take off bunt sign, but not my *cabeza*. Head, to you, amigo." He shook off the first-aiders and began walking around. When he picked up his glove and put his cap back on, the crowd gave him a big burst of applause.

Mattison walked the next batter, and Rettinger signaled toward the visitors' bullpen. Pedro, however, proved to all present that his mental faculties had not been impaired one iota when he took the next ball that was hit and started the inning-ending double play around the horn.

The score was still knotted, 3-3, in the first of the ninth. Fritz Kornauer, the Colt center fielder, struck out, but reached first base when the breaking pitch got by the Albuquerque catcher. Up for the fourth time, Frank sacrificed Kornauer to second, and Rettinger sent Eddie Mutino out to hit for Mattison. Frank, toweling the sweat off his face in the dugout, wondered why the numbers three and one on the back of the shortstop's uniform seemed to embody a certain meaning. Thirty-one. Maybe they suggested that moment of truth, the age when ballplayers have to have it made—or else.

The short rest had apparently sharpened Eddie's reflexes, Frank thought, when the shortstop swung at a fast ball that was almost by him and singled Kornauer in for the lead run. A favorite throughout the circuit, Pedro

Sanchez stepped in showered by applause, and hit the second pitch served up to him into the Pueblo first baseman's mitt. Eddie Mutino slid back to the bag but was out by an eyelash.

Rettinger's southpaw reliever, "Cookie" Jarman, mopped up in a hurry, striking out the last two men to face him, and the Colts brought their fourth straight win into the showers. Pablo Sanchez took the trainer by the arm and pointed at his brother. "My one beeg headache, *amigo*. You take care of him *pronto?*"

"Si," Pedro complained. "I have headache in *cabeza* meant for a *caballo*. That ees horse in Eengleesh."

Most of the team was dressed and ready to leave when a short, bulky man with iron-gray hair and horn-rimmed spectacles came into the long, narrow room. Rettinger, who had just ordered Webling to get Pedro to the hospital for observation, called out, "Del, you old horse thief. They got you slumming again?" He gave the players around him a sweeping glance. "This is Del Schupp, one of Milwaukee's talent scouts. Don't get excited, though. This guy doubts that even Picasso was a pro."

"Sure," Schupp said, grinning, "I've looked at so many flashes in the pan I can't count 'em, men. Why do you think I had to get cheaters at the age of thirty-nine?"

Rettinger snorted. "Del, you umpired at the battle of Vicksburg," he said.

Schupp ignored the remark and gave the Colts an overall appraisal as if they were so many samples of horse flesh. Frank, although there never had been a smattering of egotism in him, was certain the scout gave him more than a full share of scrutiny, but it did not take him more than a few seconds to realize that Schupp had one certain name written down in his book. "I seldom believe Cass," he said to Eddie Mutino, "but I have to believe his report on you. Anyway, part of it. What's Riordan hitting for Denver? Two-four-seven? Don't drop two many points off your two-six-four, Eddie, the rest of the way and maybe . . ." He turned toward the Colt manager. "If you're ready, Cass, you're coming over to the hotel with me. There's something I have to talk over with you."

"Look, Del, the Denver pitching is shaky and I know it. If you're going to raid this club just when its getting momentum and——"

"Who pays your salary, Cass?"

"I'll be right with you," the Austin pilot said. "You all hit the hay early," he threw at the Colts. "We ride to Amarillo in the morning. We play a doubleheader on Sunday."

NINE

THE COLTS LEFT ALBUQUERQUE LATE THE NEXT MORN-
ing without Pedro Sanchez, who, if he got a clean bill of
goods at the hospital, would join the club in Amarillo.
Pablo tapped Cass Rittinger on the shoulder before
boarding the bus. "Is waste of time, señor, leaving Pedro
here. They weel just look in his head an' find notheeng!"

The manager revealed the result of his talk with the
scout a few hours earlier. Pitcher Tod Billip would
report to the Denver Steers immediately after the Austin
road trip. The writers were already pounding out the
news for that day's consumption. "That scout, he does
not even look one eye at me or Pedro," Pablo Sanchez
griped. "I have the good mind to queet bezball an' go
back raising the coffee beans."

"If you had a good mind you'd never have left the
coffee patch," Hog Wilding threw almost the length of

the bus. "I got el big idea, Pablo. We go in business as partners. I raise the pork and you the beans."

It was another torrid day, but the streamlined bus was air-conditioned. Cass came up the aisle to where Eddie Mutino sat, spoke to the shortstop for a few moments, then directed Ky Webling to thin down the cool air coming out of the machine. "We're not shipping sides of beef, Ky, and I don't want half the club getting the sniffles."

Frank looked up from his magazine when the manager returned to his seat up front. Johnny Hagerman, sitting next to him, kept his voice down. "I thought it was just about right in here, around sixty degrees. I don't get it, Frank. Seems that it was all on Eddie's account. But I didn't notice him kicking about it."

"I thought the scout was kind of partial to him, too," Frank said, and went back to his reading, but the words on the printed page began to get meaningless. Turning his attention to the drab scenery of the Texas Panhandle slipping at over fifty miles per hour past the window, he wondered just how much a man had to do to be recommended for Triple A ball, for his hitting was better than that of most second basemen in the league and he had driven in more than his share of runs, considering his spot in the batting order. Maybe he had too much of a retiring personality and should have tooted his horn along with Ben long ago.

Tod Billip's voice reached him when the bus slowed down at a railroad crossing. "Like I said, Cass, don't pitch me unless you have to, because that Denver club might change their minds if I get clobbered in Amarillo or San Antone."

"We're going to get one more win out of you, Tod," Rettinger said. "Maybe two. You're resting all day today and part of tomorrow. After the Dukes we have an open date, and then——"

"You have the very hard heart like the stepsmother me an' Pedro had, señor," Pablo interrupted, "an' like you she smoked the very bad-smelling *cigarros.*"

"I like you, too, Pablo," Rettinger shot in return, "so much I would never part with you."

"Me an' my *boca grande,*" the outfielder sighed, and slumped lower into his seat.

Rettinger started pitcher-coach Lennie Otteler against the fourth place Amarillo Dukes in the first game of the doubleheader, and the sidearm specialist took a three-run lead into the last of the fourth, when the roof began to break up over his head. After retiring the first Duke batter, he walked the next two, and then Eddie Mutino had to go deep in the hole to cut off a smash by the Amarillo cleanup hitter, and his throw to first was short, pulling Hog Wilding off the bag. The bases were loaded, or as the Sanchez brothers would say, "The little pillows are congested and the launcher ees in bad trobble." The Austin bullpen got busy. A single drove in two runs, but Frank pulled Otteler out of a worst inning when he speared a low line drive off his shoe-tops and doubled the Duke base runner off first.

Hog Wilding opened the fifth inning with a screaming triple down the alley between center and right, but Kornauer struck out. Frank threw the loaded bat away and stepped up to the plate, the Duke bench jockeys on him, making flip remarks about his bowlegs. He worked the count two and two, then caught hold of a slip-pitch and sent it deep enough to right to allow Hog to tag up and score after the catch. It was his thirty-seventh run batted in. Rettinger gave him a small grin of approval when he returned to the bench. He began to wonder about Eddie Mutino a few moments later when the short-stop dribbled a pitch just inside the third base line. The Duke hot corner man had to come in halfway to scoop it up but nearly got Eddie at first.

"You tell him," Pablo Sanchez said to the Colt pilot, "he carries too much chew tobacco an' eet slows him up."

Otteler looked at a third strike and the Colts took the field with a 4-2 lead. The first Amarillo hitter, a fast man, drag-bunted himself on, and then the next batter hit a grounder a few feet to Eddie Mutino's right. The short-stop made the pick-up, hesitated for a moment, then threw to second, too late. Frank, before he threw the ball into Otteler, stared at Eddie, a question in his eyes. The Amarillo front runner had started with the pitch. A good throw to first would have at least cut down one man. Eddie just walked back to his fielding position, eyes on the ground.

Otteler threw a slider to the third man up for the Dukes and then he turned and watched the ball kick up dust inside the right field foul line. The two-base knock sent a man in and left runners on second and third. It brought the partisan crowd to its feet and sent Rettinger out to the hill. He gave the bullpen the distress signal and Cookie Jarman came walking in. While the fireman threw his quota of warmups, Frank moved over close to Hog. "I'd say Eddie needed a longer rest," he said.

"You'd better let Cass be the judge of that, Frank." Hog stooped down and picked up a pebble and threw it out on the grass. "Something's sure botherin' the guy."

Jarman nearly had the pinch hitter the Austin pilot sent up to the plate, but the man drove a three and two delivery to straightaway center, the Duke runner on third scoring on the sacrifice fly. The runner at second slid into third just a split second before Pablo Sanchez's great throw slapped into Acerbo's glove. Jarman missed both the plate and his catcher with a breaking pitch and the fifth run crossed the plate for Amarillo. The Austin fans screamed for more, and the batter obliged by hitting Jarman's third pitch over the left field fence. Johnny Hagerman met Rettinger at the mound, and Hog came over from first. Cass asked Jarman for the ball, and Hog said, "Sometimes it is the way Cookie crumbles."

Left-hander Earl Rapp, not too long out of the Panhandle sandlots, came in to put out the fire, but not before he had loaded the bases and put more gray at Rettinger's temples.

The Colts got a run in the eighth on a walk, an infield out, and a single off Frank's bat, but that was as far as they could go in the curtain raiser. During the intermission, after the Colts had sprayed their sweat and grime off, Rettinger told Bernie Jewell he would play short in the nightcap. Frank saw Eddie Mutino getting into his street clothes down at the far end of the room and nodding in reply to something Rettinger was telling him. He was certain the manager was not mentioning that error of omission on the part of the shortstop that had helped Otteler to an early shower. He caught himself feeling sorry for Eddie, and quickly asked himself why. The shortstop had the inside track on the ball club and all signs pointed to his taking a short cut to faster company.

An hour later the patched-up left side of the Colt infield fell apart at the seams, both Acerbo and Jewell missing hot grounders—the kind that Pedro Sanchez and Eddie Mutino could always put in their pockets—and Ownie Mattison found himself in the bottom of the fourth inning with two Dukes on the bases and nobody out. A left-handed pull-hitter was at the plate, and

98

Frank shifted to his right, along with Rettinger's outfielders. Hog Wilding was playing back, close to the line, when the batter smashed a wicked grounder his way. The first baseman made a great stop and threw a bullet to Bernie Jewell covering second for one out, but the shortstop's return throw went five feet over Hog's head, and a run scored. It left an Amarillo runner on second with only one out.

After Mattison had thrown a pitch to the next Duke hitter, Frank noticed that the base runner on second was getting a little reckless with his lead, and he made certain signs known to Ownie and Johnny Hagerman. The pitcher fired one outside, and Frank hopped toward the bag and took the catcher's throw, and the Duke base runner was picked off. Ownie grinned out at Frank, and with the pressure off, he reared back and fanned the Amarillo catcher.

"A heads-up play, Frank," Rettinger said when the Colts came in to swing lumber, then clapped his hands and asked for some runs. Johnny Hagerman led off for the Colts with a single through the middle, and Pablo Sanchez, after working the count to two balls and two strikes, got the pitch he liked and hit it for three bases.

Art Penovi said as Hagerman scored, "How are you going to keep Pablo out of the big leagues?"

"It's easy," the Austin trainer said with a wry smile. "There are many ways. I could name a couple."

Frank, at the bat rack, did not care to hear what they were. On more than one occasion Tom Thorp had intimated that there were politics in every walk of life, even in the game of baseball, and that a man's temperament, if negative to any degree, could hold him back more than a low batting average. Sure, there had been many miscarriages of justice in the courts of human relations. Thorp's only recipe for a ballplayer's success was keeping the lips buttoned and getting base hits when they were needed.

When Hog Wilding popped out to the infield, Frank took over in the on-deck station and watched the pitches the Duke pitcher threw at Kornauer. The man seemed to be relying on the nickel-curve, known as a slider to modern baseball buffs. The Colt center fielder swung at one for a third strike, kicked up a lot of dirt and returned to the bench. Frank dug himself a good foothold in the batter's box, looked over the first two pitches and judged them right. Ahead two and nothing, he swung at the next offering, a slider, and poked it over short for his first hit of the nightcap. He died on first when Bernie Jewell rolled feebly to the Duke pitcher.

Goose eggs prevailed for both sides until the bottom of the eighth, when Tony Acerbo raced in to field a bunt and picked up nothing but a few sprigs of grass. After the next Duke hitter struck out, Mattison walked a man. A throwing error by Bernie Jewell filled the bases, and a single by a Duke pinch hitter put Amarillo out in front, 3-2. Rettinger yanked Mattison and brought in Cookie Jarman. Three pitches later Frank got in front of a ground ball and engineered the twin killing that got the Colts out of the inning. Running into the dugout he wondered if a scout had stopped off in Amarillo for a few hours.

Leading off for the Colts, Tony Acerbo compensated for some bad fielding with a ringing single through the hole at short. Penovi brought a note of relief to the roar of the Amarillo fans by fouling off a third attempt to lay one down. Johnny Hagerman, however, powdered the first pitch thrown to him to the right field corner, and Acerbo, a fast runner, came all the way around. The fans screamed at the Amarillo pilot to put Pablo Sanchez on, and when the slugger had gotten ahead three and one the manager did decide to give the hitter a free ticket. Frank observed through a grin, "That'll burn Hog. Something tells me he'll break it up right here."

The big first baseman turned and glared at the umpire when a strike was called against him. He fouled one off, refused to be suckered by a waste pitch, then swung from his heels at a fast ball. Frank knew by the wicked crack of the bat that the Duke outfielders could do nothing but wave good-bye to the ball. It cleared the fence in left center, and three runs poured across the plate. Austin, 6, Amarillo, 3. The Colts ganged around Hog when he reached the bench and playfully cuffed him around. "In the business I got back home, I'm supposed to bring home the bacon," he said.

After Kornauer was thrown out, Frank got a handle-hit to short left, but Bernie Jewell ended the agony for the local fans by looking at a third strike. Cookie Jarman, faring much better than he had in relief in the first game, retired the Dukes in order in the last of the ninth, and gave Rettinger an even split for the afternoon.

That night, after seeing a movie with Art Penovi, Frank returned to the hotel to find Cass Rettinger in serious conversation with Eddie Mutino just inside the entrance. The manager glanced his way quickly and then lifted himself out of a big chair. "Okay, Eddie," he said to the shortstop, "supposin' we sleep on it for the next few days."

"Right, Cass," Eddie said, and Frank, when the short-stop glanced up at him, was reminded of a kid that had been caught with his hand in the cookie jar. He said, "We missed you out there in that second game."

The shortstop grinned his thanks. When he got up from his chair he seemed to be groping for something to say. Frank broke the uncomfortable silence by asking him how he was coming along with his metabolism, and the shortstop managed a grin. "Oh, it'll get out of its slump," he said, and turned and walked toward the elevators. Art Penovi came over from the newsstand and said to Frank, "That conference broke up awfully fast. Must have pretty private, top security."

"That might be Eddie's trouble, Art. Some people never feel secure."

"No kidding? How about us? Any bush leaguer that never even got a five-dollar bonus."

Frank shook his head. "I just can't figure things out. There's something eating Eddie, and——"

"He's not your worry."

Frank agreed at the moment. A few hours later, with sleep escaping him, he was not absolutely sure.

Pedro Sanchez arrived in Amarillo an hour before game time the next night, and his brother was the first to ask about his health. "I bet it was big camera they looked through your *cabeza* weeth," he said. "You got peectures?"

"Only slight contusion like I told the boss, Pablo," Pedro said, grinning, and took his uniform out of his locker. He spotted Tod Billip and hurried to congratulate him. "Triple A, amigo, si? I read in *periodico* on way." He made the rounds, greeting all the Colts as if he'd been gone a year. He slapped Frank on the rear. "How's bes' second pillow man in Tehano league?"

The heat wave still gripped the Panhandle. It was close to a hundred on the thermometer when the game got under way. Tod Billip, fighting nerves, got into trouble in the last of the first inning by walking the first two men to face him. The Duke bench let him have every rib in their book between pitches, suggested that he keep a bag packed when he got to Denver. Frank yelled in at Billip, "Keep 'em low and we'll get 'em out!" One ball and one strike later the batter hit to short, where Eddie Mutino gobbled it up and threw to Frank, who relayed it to Hog for the typical Colt double play. The Duke runner on third died there when the next batter skied to Pablo Sanchez.

It evolved into a nerve-wracking pitching duel between Billip and the Duke ace, Bill Jiordan. At the end of seven the scoreboard was a double row of zeros. Art Penovi led off the top of the eight with Austin's third hit, and Johnny Hagerman sacrificed him to second, where Pablo Sanchez picked him up with a double down the right field line. Hog Wilding popped up and Kornauer struck out, and then Billip went out to the hill to protect the one-run lead. He got the first Duke hitter to ground out to Frank, and then Eddie Mutino tried to throw out the next man from deep short and fired it low and past Hog at first. The base runner legged it to second.

Tod Billip, visibly disturbed, threw two pitches off the plate, and Frank ran in to talk to him. The pitcher asked, "What's happened to that kid's arm? For the past week, he's——"

"Just hang in, Tod," Frank said, and trotted back to his position.

Billip, his reputation on the line, called on all his good stuff and control and struck the last two men out, and fifteen minutes later the Colts galloped toward the showers with a 1-0 win.

They took the long ride to San Antonio the next day, and that night just before he was about to turn in at the Blue Bonnet Hotel, Frank heard a disturbance outside, not too far down the hall. Art Penovi, already in bed, sat up and cocked his head to listen. Frank shrugged and threw off his robe. "Maybe Cass breaking up a rummy game," he said. "It's five minutes to curfew."

Eddie Mutino showed up for breakfast with a patch of adhesive tape on his chin and a small swelling on his lower lip, and Tony Acerbo, who roomed with him on the road, hastily explained that the shortstop had tripped over a chair on his way to get a glass of water. "He went out cold," the infielder said, "and I had to send for Ky."

Frank wondered if he hadn't been blessed with an overgrown imagination as he studied the shortstop's face. Eddie, as he circled the table with his eyes, seemed to defy all present to doubt the story they had heard. The second baseman suddenly discovered that his scrambled eggs had lost their taste.

Acerbo said, a trace of irritation in him, "So who believes anybody runs into a door or—all right, I beat Eddie up."

Eddie Mutino laughed louder than all the others.

TEN

THE COLTS SPLIT THE TWO GAMES WITH THE SAN ANTO-
nio Dons, and as the bus rolled homeward Frank was
certain they would have taken both but for a lapse in the
field on the part of Eddie Mutino. In the sixth inning of
the getaway game, the Dons' first baseman, with two out
and a man on first, had hit one deep to Eddie, but the
shortstop had made no effort to get the ball over to Hog
Wilding. Given a life, the Dons had scored the run that
had made the difference. Pedro Sanchez, earlier in the
game, had made a longer throw from back of third and
had nailed his man. There was no longer any doubt in
Frank's mind that Eddie was wilting under pressure.

Frank lived alone in the capital city, in a big furnished
room on the northern perimeter. Two hours after the
team's arrival he read the sports pages of the *Austin
Record,* particularly the column labeled "Sports Whirl."

Lew Byers opined that the Colts would have little chance to win the flag without Tod Billip. A weakened pitching staff and a usually tight defense showing signs of cracking were Cass Rettinger's two big problems. The pitcher Hank Suda, just sent down from Boise by the parent club, had a record anything but impressive even against Class A hitters.

"Perhaps the most underrated player on the Colts," Byers had written, "is second baseman Frank Hyatt. Day in and day out he has been a consistent performer both in the field and at the plate. Perhaps he should be less unassuming and more of a 'holler guy' and get his light out from under the proverbial bushel. The Colts play eleven games at home, with Fort Worth coming in tomorrow night. The league leaders will undoubtedly start their ace southpaw, Pat Monahan, against . . ."

Frank laughed to himself as he put the newspaper aside, and wondered if he was not justified in clipping Byers' column and sending it to the Milwaukee front office anonymously. In his mind he paraphrased some text from the Bible. *All those bearing a reasonable amount of talent should sound their trumpets before them.*

He received a letter from Tom Thorp the next morning telling him he was doing fine, and not to forget that in the next couple of weeks the Milwaukee scouts would be nosing around the bushes for final appraisal of potential major league talent. "Just keep hustling, Frank," he concluded. "They'll just have to notice you."

Fort Worth swept both games under the lights and dropped the Colts five and a half games off the pace. They hammered Hank Suda, Billip's replacement, for six runs in the first two innings of the second game, and added seven more against Rettinger's relief corps. During both contests, Eddie became fully aware of the fact that Pedro Sanchez had been covering much of Eddie Mutino's territory, and that the second baseman never strayed too far to the left of his position. Why, he asked himself, didn't Rettinger insist upon a check-up of the shortstop?

Moving into August, the Colts were playing little better than five hundred ball and were on the verge of slipping into third place. On the day the El Paso Sun Devils rode into Austin, Frank got a call from Cass Rettinger. He was to report to the manager at the ball park an hour earlier than the rest of the Colts. Hanging up the phone he wanted to believe he was about to be pushed upstairs, but the tone of Rettinger's summons had been anything but reassuring.

Cass was sitting in an old swivel chair in his pocket-sized office just off the Colt dressing room when Frank walked in, and the second baseman had no trouble reading the signs. Rettinger hadn't touched a match to the cigar he was chewing on, and there was not even the shadow of a smile on his sun-baked face. "Take a seat, Frank," he said.

The ballplayer nodded, cleared some papers from a straight-backed chair and sat down. Rettinger chewed up his cigar another inch and said, "Frank, I have to make an experiment. Shift you over to short and give Eddie a crack at second. The kid—well, he tires about this time of year and can't make most of the long throws. He——"

"Cass," Frank interrupted, "Shortstop never was my cup of tea. I'd never get used to that position in less than a year, if ever."

"Look, Frank, I can't gamble with Bernie Jewell at short for the rest of the season. Eddie played second base in Legion and Class A ball. I know you could adjust. It would be rough for the first few games, but I want you to go along with me."

Frank shook his head, his eyes beginning to heat up in the face of Rettinger's steady glance, determined this time to hold his ground. "You're the boss, Cass. Is this an order?"

"I don't want to think of it in that way, but I run this club, Frank, with a free hand. I want Eddie Mutino in the lineup and if I have to I'll go along with Bernie Jewell."

Frank got to his feet. "This isn't exactly playing fair, Cass! I've earned that job with a pretty good bat, and you can ask Lew Byers of the *Record*. I think I've got a lot of the fans behind me, too. I'm going out on a limb and risking a bus ticket to the lower bushes with one question. Why are you willing to louse up an infield and maybe lose the pennant because of your partiality to one man in this club?"

Rettinger's eyes blazed for a moment and he took the cold cigar from his mouth and slammed it into a wastebasket. For a few charged moments Frank felt the skids under him—and well-greased. All at once Rettinger's anger left him and he fell back in his chair and wearily passed a hand over his eyes. "All right, all right, I have to do it," he said in a half-whisper. "I owe you an explanation, although it will mean breaking a confidence." He went to the door, looked out, then slammed it tight. When he returned to his chair he seemed almost angry again. "If you ever breathe a word of what I'm going to tell you, Frank, I'll see to it that you go so far out in the sticks you'll have to get your mail by horseback. Eddie is on borrowed time. He knows he cannot live much past thirty-five."

Frank's heart skipped a few beats and he felt as if he had caught the swing of a heavy bat in his stomach. "No, Cass," he choked out.

"Yes, Frank. When he was a youngster he got a strep throat and it caused damage to his kidneys that could not be repaired." The Austin manager put a fresh cigar between his teeth, and as quickly got rid of it. "I've never known a man with as many guts. He told me that sometimes he plays feeling as if there was a bag of cement tied to his back and lead weights in his shoes. One time I asked him to let all you other guys know it and he just laughed and said you all had troubles of your own." Rettinger choked up and he quickly swung his eyes away from his second baseman.

Frank's eyes were beginning to fill when Rettinger got control once more. "The other day Eddie said he'd never stop being thankful for the years of baseball he's had, that life was short enought without fouling it up with resentment. And he said that they're learning more about curing people every day and he might beat the dark angel yet."

"I wish I-I'd k-known," Frank said.

"That other night," the manager said, "the kid did not fall over anything. He just passed out. You know something, Frank? He never has asked me to take him out of a game once? There were times when I watched him that a knife was cutting through my heart, when I knew he was playing on nerve alone. Now, you are one of a few people who know about this."

Frank nodded. He wiped his eyes with a handkerchief. "Cass, you put Eddie at second."

"You won't regret it," Rettinger said. "We want Eddie to get to Class AAA before the season's over, and we'll do it in any way we can, even if we are careless with the truth and need to connive. He knows that it is just about as far as he can go and he has set his sights on it. You know something else, Frank? He knows he has shortened his life by over five years playing this game. He told me it was worth it."

There was very little more either of them could say. Frank glanced at his watch. "I think I'll take a walk, Cass, until seven o'clock."

A block from the ball park he had to admit to a certain truth, that what was one man's gain was another's misfortune, and when Tom Thorp came to his mind he was sure the man would have to admit that some sacrifices were completely justified and were essential to a man's conscience and peace of mind. Be that as it may he had to ask why he was the one generally caught right in the middle, and then a small inner voice asked him how he would like to be Eddie Mutino.

He hoped that what Cass had told him was not showing in his eyes when he approached Eddie in the dressing room and gave him his widest grin. "So we change over tonight, scatter-arm," he said. "I think we both should wish each other luck."

"Frank, it wasn't my idea," Eddie said.

"Who even thought it was?" Frank took his uniform out of the locker and tossed it to the bench. "I didn't hear they made you the manager." When he was suited up he isolated himself the best he could from the other Colts and groped for what knowledge he had of playing the shortstop position. His experience there had been confined to Indiana sand lots, and he had retained little of the text from a baseball instruction book Tom Thorp had given him on his tenth birthday. The shortstop has a wide range of territory, and more often than not, after knocking a ball down, he has little time to set himself before he throws. He has to get the ball away sidearm or overhand. Generally he has to field a ball on the run, and there is one play that occurs in almost every game that shortstops dread, the ball that is hit over second base in such a way that the shortstop has to make a long and hurried throw. And there is the fly ball that's hit over second but too close in for an outfielder to make the play.

A good shortstop gives signals to his outfielders for every ball delivered by the pitcher, and whenever a waste ball is called for by the catcher, the shortstop should be ready to cover second base if the batsman is a right-handed hitter and an attempt is made to steal second base. A tall man, everything considered, has an advantage at that position, and Frank could not qualify in that respect.

Cass Rettinger came along and said, "Relax, Frank. You know most of the hitters in this league and where they generally hit the ball. I've always maintained that most infielders, with the exception of the first baseman, can handle three positions."

He gave the manager a small smile. "I'll stop 'em from going through somehow, Cass."

There were little more than a thousand fans on hand when the Colts took the field against the Sun Devils, and when Frank went out to short he knew most of them were taking a second look at the Austin lineup on their score cards. They began yelling at Rettinger, asking him why the shake-up. Frank, when the first El Paso batter walked to the plate, sleeved sweat from his face. Pedro Sanchez came over to him. "Thees is loco, amigo. Why does Cass swap you over?"

"Ours not to reason why, Pedro," Frank shot back, and glanced toward Eddie. The converted second baseman gave him a big grin and flashed a good luck sign with thumb and forefinger, and the tightness came up into Frank's throat. Eddie looked like a man who had the world by the tail on a downhill pull instead of one who would never know whether or not life really began at forty. His right cheek lumpy from a load of scrap tobacco, Eddie Mutino was talking it up to Ownie Mattison, who was on the mound busily rubbing up a new ball.

Frank nodded to himself. He could put all his worries and frustrations out there in the middle of the diamond along with those of all the players and fans, and he would lose little time picking his up again and running away with them. Compared with Eddie he was riding the luxury section on the gravy train.

Mattison got the Sun Devils out in order to start the game, and Eddie ran into the bench, thankful no balls had been hit his way. The fans gave the Colts the whip, lashing out first at Pedro Sanchez, who turned at the plate and tipped his hat to his tormentors. The Colombian then hit the first pitch through the middle for a single and quickly changed the thin crowd's mood. The Sun Devil right-hander, Limanski, walked Art Penovi and then hit Hagerman on the arm with a pitch that sailed. Pablo Sanchez hit two long fouls, hung in until the count was full, and brought the thin crowd up yelling like ten times their number with a screaming triple down the alley in right.

Hog Wilding grounded out deep to the El Paso first baseman, and Pablo scored the Colt's fourth run. After Kornauer fanned, Frank stepped in and hit a Texas Leaguer into short left, but Eddie Mutino lined out to right.

Frank got his first fielding chance of the game in the top of the second, a slow grounder to the left of the mound he had to charge. His throw was hurried and underhand and Hog Wilding leaped high to pull it down, but the Sun Devil hitter crossed the bag before Hog came to earth again. With one out, Mattison worked on another left-handed slugger, keeping his pitches low and on the outside corner of the plate. He got his man to slam a grass-cutter to Eddie Mutino's right, and Frank got to the keystone sack to take Eddie's quick throw. He fired to Hog, then discovered that his foot had not been on the bag for the force on the front runner. A few moments later a single drove a run in for El Paso. On his way in to the bench the crowd gave it to him once over, but not too lightly.

"All right," Rettinger said, "you got a couple of rocks out of your system, Frank. Don't let it get you down."

The Colts clung to their 4-1 lead until the sixth. With two out in the top of the inning, the Sun Devil third baseman hit a short fly into shallow left, and Frank raced out onto the grass. Pablo Sanchez came running in at top speed from left, yelling that he would take the ball, but the fans drowned out his voice. Frank made a stab with his glove just as Pablo's one hundred and ninety-five pounds hit him, and all of a sudden the ball park blacked out.

He found himself in a sitting position when the lights came on for him again, looking up into Ky Webling's face. He heard Pablo ask, "Amigo, you hokay?" He got up, still gasping for air, when Rettinger took him by the arm. The right side of his head felt as if it had been tagged by Dempsey in his prime, and his stomach ached. He walked off between the manager and the trainer, getting anything but sympathy from the stands. When he eased himself to the bench he saw that a Sun Devil was leading off second. He felt no pressure of blame from the

113

reserves on the bench, and knew he read their minds correctly. Why had Cass put him in at short in the first place?

Ownie Mattison took some of the turmoil out of Frank by getting out of the inning unscathed, with the help of a sensational stop by Eddie Mutino. Pablo Sanchez, after taking on water, leaned over Eddie. "Hokay, so you do not hear me yell like big bool, but what ees wrong with your nose, amigo? Jus' before game I eat raw onion beeg as a bezball. Ha-a-a-a-a!"

Frank laughed in spite of himself and later, after three runs had poured across the plate for the Colts, he felt as if he had been taken off the hook. Ownie Mattison gave up but one more run the rest of the way, the Colts winning it, 8-2. After a shower, Frank looked into a mirror at the bruise that was coloring up on his cheekbone, and he sought out Ky Webling. The trainer said, as he put some stuff on to keep the swelling down, "He looked good at second, Frank."

"He sure did." Frank winced a little as he essayed a grin. "But was *I* a clown?"

"You won't be there for too long, Frank."

No, Ky, but maybe just long enough to lose quite a lot of ground I've gained. He got up from the table, his nostrils twitching like a rabbit's. "Ky, was that horse liniment you used?"

"What else? What does it say across the front of your shirt?"

He was about to say "sucker," but the word tumbled back into his throat when he heard Eddie Mutino's infectious laugh. He swung around and saw the man sitting between the Sanchez brothers, an appreciative captive audience. When he reached his locker he could hear Pablo very plain. "So thees rich hombre," the left fielder

114

said, "they bury heem in Cadillac auto, an' poor ol' Pepito come by an' look an' say, 'Amigoes, that ees living, si?' Haa-a-a-a!"

Frank's blood ran suddenly cold. He desperately tried to get Pablo's attention for a moment before it occurred to him that he had to leave well enough alone. And anyway, Eddie Mutino was doubled up with laughter.

ELEVEN

THE AUSTIN SPORTS WRITER LEW BYERS USED UP MOST of his column the next day on the switch Cass Rettinger had made in the Colt infield and admitted that he was at a loss in figuring out the reason for it. Eddie Mutino had handled the second base position well enough, but Frank Hyatt certainly had looked far from home at short. "After a talk with Cass this morning, we are convinced that the Colt manager has a little Stengelese in him. It went something like this: 'You're supposed to be a smart baseball man, Lew, so maybe you have noticed or read about Eddie not gettin' the long throws over lately, so if his arm is troubling him a little I shift Hyatt to short, as I can't use Bernie Jewell every day, seein' as how he don't hit so good. I figure to go along like this for as long as Eddie's arm . . .' "

Byers' last paragraph told the fans that Milwaukee was

sending two promising Class A players to the Colts, a pitcher, Jack Corum, and an infielder, Vic Bonamo, to compensate for Tod Billip's promotion to Class AAA. Corum, a right-hander, had hung up a 12-9 record at Davenport.

After reading Byers' stint, Frank felt a shred of satisfaction. He knew something the sports writers did not know. That night, however, he wished he could have borrowed most of what Eddie Mutino knew about playing shortstop.

Rettinger started the man up from Davenport against the Sun Devils. Corum retired the first man to face him on a routine ground ball to third, then got behind the next hitter and finally walked him. Novogratz, a three hundred hitter, smashed one back of third that Pedro Sanchez knocked down but could not field, and there were runners on first and second. The Sun Devil cleanup batter took a ball, a strike, another ball, then drove the fourth pitch inside third where it squirted off Pedro's glove and rolled out into left field when Frank was slow in backing up the third baseman. It was an error of commission for Pedro, one of omission for Frank, and baseball-wise spectators yelled at him to get the lead out.

Two runs scored before Corum retired El Paso, and when he got to the bench the shortstop's eyes dared Rettinger to call him on that particular play. He had words ready for the man. *You put a square peg in a round hole, Cass, so wait until the corners are shaved off*. The manager called after Pedro, "Get us going, amigo."

Pedro washed out his error with a screaming double to the right field corner. Art Penovi popped up, but Hagerman blooped one into short right that the Sun Devil right fielder lost when he tried a shoestring catch, and Pedro came across the plate. With the Colt catcher on second,

Pablo Sanchez nailed a three and one offering down the alley between left and center, tieing up the ball game and reaching third on a belly-slide. Hog Wilding, with the crowd emulating a hog caller's cry, scored Pablo with a towering fly to deep center. The Sun Devil southpaw, after a look at the feverish action in the visitors' bullpen, steadied himself and struck out Fritz Kornauer.

Corum kept the one-run lead until the fifth, when with a Sun Devil on first and one out, the hitter scorched a grounder just inside first. Hog fielded it, touched the bag, then threw to Frank, covering second. The shortstop failed to tag the runner before firing back to first, and instead of a twin-killing there was a man on second and a good hitter in the batter's box. A few moments later, a single knotted up the ball game.

Frank kicked himself all the way into the bench when the Colts came in for their cuts, for he should have known in a situation like that that he hadn't had a force play. He snapped at Cass Rettinger, "Clear out a place here for the rocks I'm piling up."

"As long as we keep winning, Frank, they won't hurt too much," Rettinger said.

Corum, the pitcher, proved himself to be a brash rookie. "They told me at Davenport that I'd get better support in Class AA. Was that a snow job?"

"So far, amigo," Pablo Sanchez threw at the man, "you have got us *jardineros* weeth our tongues hanging way out." He held up four fingers. *"Cuatro veces,* four times you have me climbeeng the fence, si."

"Jardi—what he said," Hog told the pitcher, "means outfielders."

The score remained 3-3 until the eighth, and then the El Paso heavy artillery shelled Corum out with four straight hits, one a double that sent three runs across, and

Rettinger took the rookie right-hander out. While Cookie Jarman came walking in, Frank looked over at Eddie and read certain signs that brought an ache under his breastbone. The temperature just before the game had been between ninety and a hundred, and the flannel uniforms of both teams were heavy with sweat. Eddie's eyes were a little feverish in the artificial light, and a whiteness seemed to be spreading around his mouth. Rettinger had not exaggerated when he'd said that the man played with weights on his back.

Two minutes later, Eddie Mutino went far to his left, stopped what seemed to be a sure hit, and fired to Hog in time to get the third out. Frank saw Rettinger project a question to Eddie with his eyes when the second baseman took his place on the bench. Eddie's lips stretched out. He shook his head.

The Colts, sparked by a lead-off triple by Hog, narrowed the Sun Devil lead to a run in their half of the inning, but that was as far as they could go for the night. Taking his shower Frank knew that at least one of his rocks had been the difference.

His struggle to master reasonably the shortstop position affected his hitting, and he managed but two singles against the next two invading clubs, Albuquerque and Fort Worth. And the Milwaukee scout, Del Schupp, had been looking on when he'd booted two runs in against the Pueblos. Eddie Mutino, on the other hand, had driven out two hits in that game, and had made three great plays in the field.

Frank got a letter from Tom Thorp a few hours before the San Antonio Dons opened a two game series in Austin, and the old ballplayer had dipped his pen in gall and wormwood while blasting Rettinger. He also questioned whether or not Frank Hyatt had anything resembling a backbone, being willing to be pushed around like that to build another player up. "Even if you were willing to take it lying down, Frank," Thorp wrote, "Milwaukee's front office ought to know how their minor league players are being developed and how their clubs are managed. You have a legitimate beef against the deal you're getting, so make it!"

The reluctant shortstop wrote Thorp a brief reply, inferring that Cass Rettinger along with himself were victims of circumstances beyond their control, and although the move had been somewhat disastrous for him, he had found great satisfaction in discovering that there was a human side of baseball. Even as he mailed the letter he visualized Thorp scratching his graying head after reading it, and heard him wonder aloud if his protégé's head did not need a valve-grinding job.

Ownie Mattison, the stopper, shut out San Antonio in the series opener, 7-0. The Colts banged out thirteen hits, one of them of the scratch variety by Frank Hyatt. The one for four night dropped his batting average to .249. Peeling off his flannels, he knew that the fans would keep off his back as long as the Colts kept winning more than they lost, but if a bad slump came they would see that he sprouted the horns of a goat. Tom Thorp already had him tagged, however, as a sacrificial lamb.

The wheeling and the dealing were under way around the major league circuit the next day. When the Colts arrived at the ball park, they found Lew Byers and another writer in earnest conversation with Cass Rettinger. When the scribes left, the manager made his announcement. After the next road trip, Eddie Mutino would report to the Denver Steers to replace a shortstop going up to the majors, and Johnny Hagerman, the catcher, had been part of a Milwaukee-Cincinnati deal, and would report to the Tanagers at the close of the Texas League pennant race.

The Colts, although apparently at a loss to understand the parent club's actions, lost no time in congratulating Eddie Mutino, who during a short space of time seemed to have gained ten pounds and grown a foot taller. Their enthusiasm over Hagerman's good fortune was even more pronounced. The Sanchez brothers, feigning despair, consoled each other. "So we go to theese night school, Pedro said to Pablo, "an' learn better Eengleesh an' they weel understand we are bezball players, si. We weel make el big show."

"Have patience, amigoes," Rettinger said, "you just can't miss."

"We geet *abogado*, a lawyer, Pedro," Pablo grinned, "an' make Señor Cass put eet in the writin'."

Rettinger moved over close to Frank. "Only ten more days and you'll be back at the old stand. I want you to know I appreciate all you've——"

"I wouldn't say the fans did," Frank said, a touch of bitterness in his voice. "I've lost ground that's going to be hard to regain. Oh, I suppose the scouts took the fielding switch into consideration, but my hitting! Do they recognize a thing called a mental hazard?"

"I guess they would if they could see what was on Eddie's mind," the manager said a little impatiently.

"Yeah, Cass. Excuse me for forgetting."

Only two and a half games behind the league leaders, the Colts drew nearly four thousand fans that night. Rettinger pitched Jack Corum against the Dons. Jack was beginning to look like a Double A hurler. Neither side managed to get a base runner for the first two and a half innings. Frank, leading off to begin the Colts' bottom of

121

the third, heard a fan up front yell, "One out!" He watched the first pitch go by for a strike, and many more fans got on him. He stepped out, got dirt on his hands, and glanced over at Eddie Mutino waiting to hit. He never remembered looking at a happier face. It made him feel good and drained away what little resentment was left in him.

The San Antonio southpaw threw him a pitch with a string attached and he timed its lazy arc and smashed the ball through the hole at short for the first hit of the ball game. Eddie Mutino got the bunt sign and dumped the first pitch up the first base line, fair by not more than an inch, and the Dons' pitcher and first baseman let it roll, gambling that it would go foul. They lost, and the Colts were in business. Rettinger put the bunt sign on for Corum, but the pitcher popped it up to the mound, the Austin runners scrambling back.

Pedro Sanchez struck out, and the crowd's clamor for a big inning ran back into their throats. And then they were off their seats and howling at the Texas moon when Art Penovi hit the first pitch and drove it into the left field corner. Eddie Mutino came all the way in from first to score behind Frank, and when he got to the Colts' bench he had to struggle for breath for a few moments. Frank watched Ky Webling follow Eddie to the water cooler, put an arm around him and say something that could not be heard above the fans' delighted racket. Eddie shook his head, then lowered it to the cool water.

Johnny Hagerman drove a two and two pitch straight at the San Antonio second baseman, who let it go through his legs, and Penovi scored. Pablo Sanchez, determined to prove that Rettinger had not just been whistling "Dixie" in his appraisal of the Latin brothers, got hold of a gopher ball and hit it out of sight to give the

Colts a 5-0 bulge. Coming into the dugout, Pablo slapped Pedro on the head. "Next time ees your turn, si? You heet the ball or I heet you!"

Corum took the lead into the seventh that proved to be anything but lucky. After striking out the first batter, he lost control and walked the next two men. The pitcher due up, the Dons' manager reached for his bench. Frank concentrated on the runner at second, keeping him as close as possible to the bag, and failed to see Pedro Sanchez warning him against keeping his fielding position too open. The batter smashed a pitch through the gaping hole at short and drove in the first San Antonio run. Corum looked out at him, then kicked the rosin bag halfway to second base. Rettinger came out on the run, signaling to his bullpen. "That's all, Corum," he yelled.

The fans showered the manager with boos when he came off the field. Pedro trotted over to cheer up the shortstop. "That launcher has beeg sore in the *cabeza*, Frank. He weel never even see Triples A." He suddenly clamped his gloved hand to his head. *"Caramba,* he just poosh Señor Cass!"

Corum really was acting up in the dugout. Frank saw Rettinger open up wide against the recalcitrant pitcher, and stab a forefinger close to Corum's face. He knew the pitcher's flare-up would cost him.

Earl Rapp took over the pitching chores for the Colts and allowed the Dons but one more run on a sacrifice fly. Leading off in the Colts' half, he surprised himself even more than the fans by getting a handle hit that fell beyond the reach of the back-pedaling Don second baseman. Pedro Sanchez, after working the count full, got his first hit of the game, a *tubey* to left that sent Rapp around to third. Penovi hit into a fielder's choice, but Rapp scored on the out. Hagerman fouled out, and the Don pitcher purposely walked Pablo Sanchez. Answering the insult, Hog Wilding cleared the bases with a triple. Frank, leaving the dugout behind the next hitter, Fritz Kornauer, wondered if scouts were half intelligent. Pablo was hitting .338.

The Colts ended the home stand with an 8-2 win. Tomorrow, Saturday, they would take the bus to El Paso, where a Sabbath doubleheader was scheduled. After a shower, Frank saw Eddie taking the cap off a little bottle of pills, and the second baseman seemed to be hurrying the action, his heavy sun tan seeming to wash thin. Rettinger suddenly called out, "You got many salt pills left, Eddie?" and the second baseman nodded and gave the manager a grateful smile.

"Only four more days in Double A," Art Penovi said to Eddie. "Don't forget to remember us when."

The Colts left Austin a game and a half behind Fort Worth. They swept three from the Sun Devils, got a split with the Amarillo Dukes, and when they returned home, leading the league by a full game, they said good-bye to Eddie Mutino. Frank, Cass Rettinger, and Ky Webling, all aware that they might never see Eddie again, had to hang on to their control. When Eddie said, "I'll never forget you guys—not as long as I live," Rettinger nearly let go.

He fairly shouted at the trainer, "For the love of Mike, Ky, what do you put in that liniment you use?"

Eddie made it a point to corner Frank before he left the dressing room. "Thanks for—going along with Cass," he said, "until I got straightened around. Maybe I should tell you———"

"Get lost before you slop over," Frank almost snapped. "I just took orders."

When most of the players had gone, Frank sat down in

front of his locker and sipped at a bottle of orangeade. Cass Rettinger came out of his little office chewing on a cigar. He came over and grinned down at the infielder. "Well, Bernie Jewell will play short the rest of the way, Frank." He laughed out loud. "He couldn't play that position any worse than you."

Frank picked up a sodden sweat shirt and fired it against the wall. "Thanks, Cass, but I can't admit that was very funny. It most likely cost me another year in the bushes and——"

"Okay, Frank, I'm sorry for the crack. But believe me, some day you'll look back when you're sitting on a Big League bench, most likely in Milwaukee, and laugh over the trials and tribulations of your days in the bushes."

———

Now, on the Milwaukee bench, he was not laughing while Sam Kelso strode out to the mound to get Zach Izzro out of there. Maybe he had come here because a story had been kicked around until it landed in the Milwaukee front office that said that greater love hath no man than one who lays down his very baseball life for a friend. Maybe they would let him sit around for a while in the majors so that he could say he had reached the big show, and with winter coming spring could not be far behind. No doubt it would find him tossed back into the shuffle.

His eyes widened when he saw Danny Sloat walk to the hill and catch the ball Izzro tossed at him. When Kelso walked off, Danny nervously kicked at the dirt and kept banging the ball into his glove. The Chiefs behind him began talking it up, shouting encouragement. Al Jansky went out to talk to him, the fans griping over the delay, still stung by the home run that had tied the score at 5-5.

The rookie pitcher gave up a single to the first man to face him, then retired the next two men on easy ground balls, and he gave Frank a broad smile when he reached the bench. It was wasted on the player up from Denver, who was having nerves at the moment. Vanderpool might well get a chance at bat this half of the inning. Would Kelso stay with him?

Al Jansky worried the Metro southpaw by spraying fouls right and left, and finally drew a walk. When Eckert and Martsell failed to advance the runner, Kelso did not call Vanderpool back, and Frank lowered his head lest the Milwaukee skipper catch the slow burn in his eyes. The bonus player got behind two and one, then watched a fast ball blow past, and the Metro catcher fired to his man at third. Vanderpool had a word or two with the man in blue, then threw his hard hat away and walked toward the infield.

Danny Sloat went out there and held back the other people, one, two, three, and he got a round of applause when he led off for the Chiefs in their half. The pitcher had the fans yelling louder when he dumped a bunt just inside the first base line and beat it out. Provost also got the bunt sign, but after working the count out full, laid one down foul and was out of there. Johnny Drew forced Sloat at second, and the fans yelled for big Raneri to hit one all the way. The center fielder missed a homer by inches, then fouled out to the Metro catcher.

The visitors still were unable to break through on Danny Sloat in the top of the eleventh, and Kelso growled at his team as it came in. "Let's get a run and then some sleep."

Joe Arriga, swinging from his heels, fanned on a ball

that had a string attached, but Al Jansky responded to the crowd's demanding cry with a single to left. Eckert was safe when the Metro first baseman bobbled his third baseman's long throw, and the fans were in full cry. When Martsell left the on-deck circle, Kelso called Vanderpool back from the lumber pile. "Hyatt," he said, "get a stick!"

Waiting out there once more, Frank gathered wool that warmed him. If Martsell failed to bring a run in, it could be the moment he had often dreamed about. He saw Martsell look up at third for the sign, and the right fielder shortened up as if to bunt and had a strike called against him. Frank was certain Kelso had the bunt sign off when Martsell dug in again—Martsell's orders to slam the ball past the third baseman when he moved in on the grass. Martsell took a pitch too high, then slung at a sinker and hit into the double play.

Frank tossed his bat away and went out to take over at second, and he had hardly felt his spikes dig into Big League dirt when the first Metro hitter caught hold of Danny Sloat's fast ball and hit it into the right field seats. The one run proved to be enough for New York. The Chiefs went down in order in their half, and Frank made his way off the field still with no times at bat and without one chance in the field. The pennant race was unwinding fast and he was seeing a drab vision indeed as he peeled off for his shower. He saw brother Ben's gas station back in Indiana and a motorist was saying to a man who looked exactly like himself, "Fill 'er up, Mac."

● TWELVE

"WELL, I'VE PITCHED A COUPLE OF INNINGS IN THE BIG Leagues," Danny Sloat said when he and Frank reached their living quarters, "and who hasn't thrown a gopher ball? I believe there's a Big League manager on the coast who has won a couple of pennants, and he appeared in one ball game in the majors." He lifted his arms high and yawned. "But you know something, Frank? I'm scared just thinking of that plane trip to L.A., after this series. I've never flown." He forced a laugh. "But they say you don't go until your number is up."

Frank nodded, felt that constriction in his throat, and turned his face away from the pitcher. He was remembering the man who had worn the number 31 and who had died when he'd reached that age. "You'll take to flying like a big-tailed bird, Danny," he said, "especially after you've seen the hostesses."

He got up and crossed the room to get the late sports news on the TV. It was already on and the announcer said, ". . . and that loss to the tail-end New York Metros was a body blow to San Kelso's pennant chances. The Chiefs blew a commanding lead, the big bomb set off by Krist against reliefer Zach Izzro.

"With the pennant races practically in the stretches, many deals have been made and are in the offing, particularly on the part of contending clubs. The Chicago Bruins—and this is more than a rumor—is in the midst of a transaction with the Chiefs' front office involving three players and a certain amount of cash. The key man is Pablo Sanchez, currently hitting three forty-one for the Denver Steers. Sanchez has hit twenty-nine home runs. Early in the season last year, the slugger threatened a sit-down strike after the Milwaukee club sent his brother, Pedro, a third baseman, to the Tulsa Sooners in a deal with the Saint Louis Tanagers. The Corsairs continue to . . ."

Frank grinned as he snapped off the TV. Good old Pablo. He'll have Pedro on the same ball club with him again if he has to take his case to the United Nations.

"That Vanderpool," Danny Sloat said, as he plugged in an electric toothbrush, "sure will have to go down for a little more experience. If Duhamel is still hurting too much tonight I'll lay you three to one Kelso has you in the lineup."

"Never bet on me, Danny. I could break a leg before game time tomorrow night helping an old lady across the street."

After breakfast the next morning they went downstairs and emptied their mailbox, and Frank found a letter from Tom Thorp. Its contents brought a grin to his mouth that kept getting wider. Business at Ben's gas station had increased a good fifteen per cent since his brother had come up to the Big Leagues. "He's got photographs of you taken in Denver all over the place," Thorp wrote, "and he's changed the sign to Hyatt Bros."

"So Ben's sounding my trumpets before me," he mused aloud.

Sloat asked, "Huh? What was that, Frank?"

"Nothing, Danny." He pocketed the letter and rolled up his sleeves. "We'd better clean up two days' dirty dishes or we will have to eat right out of the pots and pans."

"They can wait, Frank. Let's eat out for a couple of days. Do you think we'll ever make ten thousand a year in this game?"

A half hour before game time, the Chiefs were taking their cuts in the batting cage. Frank sat on the bench not far from where Sam Kelso was studying his lineup for the night, watching Joe Arriga hit them hard and far against the batting practice pitcher. In the dressing room Richie Duhamel had been tagged by Sam Shugrue, the trainer, still *hors de combat* for at least another day. After Arriga, Jansky and Eckert had taken their cuts Kelso suddenly said, "Get out there, Hyatt, and hit a few."

"Looks like you play, kid," Hy Brown said, keeping his voice down.

He went out there with a bat and waited until Martsell had swung at a few. Pete Ibarra was about to step in ahead of him, then backed off. "Go ahead, Frank. I've got a blister on my hand anyway."

His heart thumped as he took his stance, choking up on the bat slightly, feeling the pressure of Kelso's eyes. The veterans ribbed him without malice as Tug Rowell turned the ball loose. Frank swung and lined it toward left and the tightness went out of him. He cut at a dozen pitches, getting a lot of good wood on most of them, and when he left the cage, Ibarra said, "You swing a pretty good banjo, kid."

The fans, no doubt willing to wait until next year, straggled in, and there were less than ten thousand looking on when the Chiefs finished infield practice behind the visiting Metros. Frank was cooling off in front of his locker when Kelso told him he would start at second base, and he nodded and then laid a grin on the floor. This was the oasis in the desert at last, he thought—a big, cool drink after the shallow water holes in the bushes. He hoped he would not choke. Vanderpool walked past, stopped, and threw over his shoulder, "Don't look too good out there tonight, Frank."

The second baseman grinned. "Maybe we could make a deal. Half your bonus money?"

The laughter that followed flushed the rookie's face, and Frank hastily added, "I'm sorry I said that."

The clock's big hand seemed to race. He wished there were at least ninety seconds in every minute. He talked to himself. Don't forget any of them: Thorp, Fred Veck, Cass Rettinger, and Bert Moger—all those men you played with. More than a little of the baseball savvy they possessed had to rub off on you. After all those years where could there be a raw spot in you? Keep saying it. Good field, pretty good hit.

He was building up his confidence, block by block, when Harry Crossett, who broadcasted the Milwaukee games both from the radio and TV side, came in with a trio of writers. He paid them little attention until Crossett raised his voice above the sound of orderly confusion. "Sam, I want you to meet George Barr. He's joining the Chiefs' public relations department, and he's up from the *Salt Lake City Register*. He's taking his first look around and . . ."

Frank drew in his breath, shook his head dolefully,

and got up to get a better look. He gently shoved Joe Arriga aside and stared at the newcomer to the Milwaukee organization, a square-faced man in his early forties, with a slightly hooked nose his outstanding feature. He moved to a far corner of the room, fretting over the fact that the world had to be as small as it was at times, and when he saw his chance he moved toward an exit that led to the dugout. Sam Kelso caught him from behind. "Frank, an old friend wants to see you."

The second baseman turned and saw Barr's grin right behind the manager's shoulder. He matched it the best he could and said tritely, "Well, what do you know?" He took the man's firm grip when Kelso walked away, and forced a smile when Barr reminiscently ran the tips of his fingers along his right jaw. "That was a real wallop, Frank, but I deserved it. It took me a long time before I could really live with myself again."

"Could I forget it, George?" It cost me an extra year in the minors, so I felt it worse than you did."

"I never could figure why you tied in with Van Etten, Frank. Was he really worth it?"

"Let's say his family was."

Barr nodded. "Whenever you're selling, I'm buying, friend. You know something, Frank? That punch put me on the wagon." He moved away, and Frank sat down on the bench next to Hy Brown. "How much time, Hy?"

"About three minutes. Stay loose, man!"

———————

In three minutes a man can review a lifetime, especially if he is still short of thirty years. . . . Frank had first run into Ray Van Etten at the Milwaukee training complex in Waycross, down in Georgia. The Chiefs had bought him right out of college, had paid him a sizable bonus, and had sent him to Class AA. The man was loaded with talent but had one weakness, a hair-trigger temper. Van Etten had been married during his junior year at Kentucky State, and had a son before he had his diploma. While being educated in the Blue Grass State the first baseman had developed a deep interest in thoroughbreds of the four-legged variety.

He arrived at the Milwaukee camp in a trailer, along with his wife, and his son, now nearly four, and when Frank met him for the first time he had the feeling that he'd known him all his life. Van Etten was a tall, broadshouldered, brown-haired man with a smile that belied the fuse that was always sputtering deep inside him. After the first workout at Waycross, Van Etten immediately sought Frank out. "You're a bachelor and far from home. Come along and have dinner with me and Pat tonight."

"You'd better call her first, Ray."

"The phone isn't hooked up. Anyway, she wouldn't expect me to."

It was little Andy Van Etten who took Frank over hook, line and sinker. He was destined to be the perfectly innocent cause of the ex-Colt's longest delay on the rocky road to the majors. He was a chubby-cheeked little guy with big, wide, brown eyes and a tuft of hair that stuck up on his head like the topknot of a kewpie doll, and he had a winning personality big enough for three little sprouts. Pat Van Etten was tall, brown-haired and long-limbed, and Frank admitted that Ray knew thoroughbreds.

Before the dinner was half ready, little Andy climbed Frank's knee with a first basemen's mitt that seemed half as big as himself on his left hand. He told Frank he was going to be a baseball player like his pop, and with Denver, too.

"You never played in Denver, did you?" Ray called from the little kitchen. "Well, it's five thousand feet up and you have to take on oxygen after running halfway around the bases. But you get used to it. You want anything stronger than root beer?"

"No," Frank said and listened to the rather garbled account of an animated cartoon movie little Andy had seen on TV. At that, he thought, he talked twice as clearly as the Sanchez brothers. Pat came out and announced that Andy's dinner was ready and she had to exercise stern parental authority to get him off Frank's knee.

The talk was mostly baseball between the tomato juice, salad, steak, and custard pie. The Van Ettens had bought the trailer with the first down payment on the bonus, and they'd live in it at Denver until they could swing a house. "I guess I was luckier than you," Ray said. "You had to really battle it from the bottom. What do you think of Bert Moger?"

"The manager? I'll bet he was a top sergeant in the Marines," Frank laughed. "I hear he's a real right Joe if you meet him halfway. But if you don't hustle, you're dead."

It was cramped in the trailer. A rubber ball came out of the bedroom and bounced off Frank's plate. Little Andy followed it in, climbed on Frank's lap again and put up a rhubarb when he was torn loose. "He certainly has taken a shine to you, Frank," Pat said, when things quieted down.

"He should be the son of a big league owner," the second baseman said.

"Give me time," Ray said.

Before he returned to the quarters assigned to the

Denver players, the Van Ettens made it quite plain that Frank was to ride back to Denver with them when he training grind broke up.

Moving up a notch in baseball meant facing better pitching, stiffer competition, and adjustment to new personalities. Dozens of men he had played with and against since the Grand Forks days—men he had practically lived with—were fast being shunted to the back of his mind to become just so many names and faces. He doubted if there was another profession in the world where a man said so many hellos and good-byes. He had to battle some good talent at Waycross, but when the exhibition games came around he was in Bert Moger's book at second base with a spring batting average of .271.

Late in April, he rode up to Denver with the Van Ettens—"Uncle Frank," as far as little Andy was concerned—and there he and third baseman Nick Saba and left fielder Hack Shellenbach rented an apartment not far from the ball park where from a mile-high altitude they could see the far sweep of the Rockies almost as far south as Pike's Peak.

The Steers opened the southern division of the Pacific Coast League against the San Diego Padres, Bert Moger starting his ace right-hander, Jim Plachette, against the Padre bell-wether, Hoot Cottrell. Running out a slow roller in the last of the second inning, Frank realized how much thinner the air was in the City Beautiful. The Padre first baseman grinned at him as he came in to hold him on. "Better take a deep breath, Mac, before you take a lead off," he said.

Steve Holovak, the Steer right fielder, hitting seventh, doubled deep to left and Frank had to go all out to reach third. With two out, Nick Saba popped up to the infield, and Frank was still breathing hard when he went out to his position. The fans began to save their collective breath when the game turned into a tight pitching duel. In the last of the seventh, the score still 0-0, Hack Shellenbach, the Denver left fielder, drew a walk with one man out. Ray Van Etten, hitting third in Bert Moger's batting order, worked Cottrell to the critical three and two count, then swung hard at a slider and got a small piece of it. The ball rolled between first base and the mound, and Cottrell went after it like a jack rabbit, scooped it up and fired to first. The throw was hurried and it hit Van Etten on the back of his hard hat and bounced toward the stands. Frank came up off the bench with the other Steers when, instead of continuing on to second, Van Etten charged toward the San Diego pitcher. Cottrell shed his glove, and his infielders came in to back him up.

Bert Moger ran out to help an umpire and his first base coach cool Van Etten off, the crowd thoroughly enjoying the first burst of excitement. No punches thrown, the Steer base runner was not thrown out. "Man, he has a short fuse," Nick Saba said, shaking his head. "Frank, how long will he last?"

The tantrum cost Denver a run, for Mike Gurstine, the center fielder and clean-up man, stroked a long single to left. Van Etten died on third when the third out was made. The Padres came in and built up a big run on a walk, a sacrifice and a single before Plachette got them out. Moger was steaming when the Steers came in, and he took his first baseman by the horns. "We lose this one, bonus man, and it'll cost you twenty-five bucks! Grab hold of that temper of yours or I'll bench you as quick as I can spit tobacco juice."

"I'm sorry, Bert," Van Etten said. "I was a knothead."

Frank had forebodings in the ninth when he watched Ray kneeling in the on-deck circle, the first baseman's ears getting red as the Padres rode him hard. A case of "rabbit-ears" could shorten a man's career. There was a runner on second, and Hack Shellenbach was at the plate. Two men were out, and the fans screamed for the run that would tie it up. Shellenbach, however, sent them home grumbling when he drove a long fly to center for the final out.

"Twenty-five bucks it is, Van Etten!" the Denver manager shouted at his first baseman when the Steers filled the dressing room. "Next time, fifty! You got that?"

"Okay, okay, Bert! How about me opening a charge account?"

Frank, when he got into the shower room, moved next to Ray and yelled above the downpour, "You've got to knock it off, Ray. The fans, the other clubs, they'll work on you if——"

"Yeah, Frank. I know."

The second baseman, little Andy in mind, kept on Ray as they got into street clothes. "You create a certain image, Ray, and it follows you all the way through your career. You've got a kid that thinks you're a knight on a big white horse, and if you louse things up it'll break his heart. And Pat, she——"

Van Etten said, "Sure, I really have got to watch it."

The second baseman was mildly satisfied with his debut in Triple A ball. He'd managed a hit off Cottrell in three official trips to the plate and he'd had four assists and one put-out.

A crazier setup than the ten teams in the two divisions of the Pacific Coast League could hardly be imagined. They traveled by plane, bus and on the rails, and they worked from San Diego in the deep southwest to Hawaii;

to Tacoma, Seattle and Portland in the northwest; and then on down to Dallas and Oklahoma City, with Salt Lake City somewhere in between. Like all minor league teams they played mostly at night. The Steers won three straight after losing the opener, lost one to Salt Lake, then swept three from Oklahoma City. When Frank boarded a plane with the rest of the Steers, destination Seattle, he was hitting .278.

Frank sat with Ray. As the plane became airborne, he suddenly laughed. "That Andy. The other night he heard you telling Pat you were going to try that poi when you got to Hawaii, and he asked me was it pineapple poi. You know that kid has got quite a throwing arm, Ray, for his age. How far away was he when he broke that neighbor's window?"

"He sure is nuts about you, Frank."

In Tacoma, in the top of the fifth, with the Steers ahead, 4-3, Ray, with the count two and two, watched a low pitch go by, and the umpire called it strike three. The first baseman slammed his bat down and put his jaw close to the plate umpire's nose and asked the man if he had ever heard of bifocals. Quickly he got eviction orders, and when the Tacoma catcher made a certain remark he seemed about to strip the man of his tools. Bert Moger came out of the dugout and roared, "Knock it off, you rockhead!"

When Van Etten took himself away for the night, Frank stared down at his feet, wondering if he had cottoned to the wrong man.

● THIRTEEN

WHEN SUMMER OFFICIALLY MOVED IN AND BEGAN WARM-
ing the high peaks of Colorado the Steers had the hottest
club in the Coast League's southern division and the
choicest source of copy for the sports writers, namely,
Ray Van Etten. Despite Frank's continued attempts to
restrain him he was a powder keg on spikes, ready to
explode at the most unexpected moments. It never occurred to him nine times out of ten to weigh certain
words before he turned them loose, and he was ready at
all times when tension built up to take on Joe Louis and
John L. Sullivan at one and the same time. He kept up
his insurance against being demoted to Double A with a
.368 batting average.

"Try to hold him down, Frank," Pat Van Etten told
the second baseman a few hours before the Steers opened
a three-game set with the Portland Chicks. "Talk to him

cold turkey." With little Andy hanging on to one of his legs, Frank promised that he would try.

When the Denver players wound up infield practice that night, Frank saw Ray go over to a field box and talk with two men for a few moments. They were, in his book, a pair of "sharpies," and when he got to the dugout, Mike Gurstine, the Steer center fielder and an ex-big leaguer, said, "You'd better tell your pal to keep away from Vinnie Disko. It is rumored he would fix anything for a buck or two and I don't mean a clock radio."

Frank glanced toward Bert Moger, glad to see that the manager was engrossed in figuring out his batting order for the night. The writers, however, seldom missed any little side-actions in the ball park, for these often were the ingredients for a good story. Van Etten came to the bench and Frank maneuvered him toward the drinking fountain. "Where did you meet those characters?" he asked.

"Around," Ray said, and turned and glared at the second baseman. "Look, I don't need a keeper, Frank."

"Forget it."

Moger started Leo Bourk against the invading Chicks, a left-hander with a wicked curve ball, and almost unbeatable when he could control it. This promised to be one of his wild nights when he walked the first two men to face him. Van Etten came over to the mound and said something to Bourk that reddened the hurler's neck. He snapped something at the first baseman, then slammed down the rosin bag as if it had suddenly held a scorpion. A small group of fans, either hostile or neutral, got on Van Etten when he returned to his position.

Bourk got the third Chick hitter to drive one to Frank's left, and he cut it off, whirled, and fired to Phil Scully, covering second. Scully to Van Etten, and there were two out and a runner on third. Bourk grinned out at Frank, then worked carefully on the Portland cleanup hitter and finally struck him out. When he got to the bench he said to Van Etten, "Look, bonus wonder, don't tell me how to pitch."

"Knock it off," Moger ordered, when the first baseman's eyes flashed the danger sign.

The game stayed tight, 1-1, until the top of the sixth, when the Chicks got two men on with a walk and a throwing error on the part of Scully at short. With one out, a good bunt advanced both runners, and a sacrifice fly put the Chicks ahead, 2-1. Phil Scully made the fans forget his error by leading off the Steers' half with a double to left, and Shellenbach sent him to the pick-up station with a drag bunt he almost beat out. The crowd became full-voiced for the first time when the hard-hitting Steer first baseman stepped up to hit. With two out, Van Etten swung from his heels at the first two pitches. He took a ball, then took a good cut when the Chick pitcher gave him a big motion and a ball that just floated in. He swung far ahead of it, then fired his bat away, nearly taking legs out from under the batboy. Boos followed him out to the field.

The Portland right-hander would not let the Steers break out of the corral, and Bourk lost a heartbreaker, 2-1. Mike Gurstine said to Van Etten in the dressing room, "He sure suckered you, Ray. You should've expected that pitch after he threw those bullets at you."

"Mike, you're such a smart hitter, why couldn't you stay with fast company?" Van Etten turned away and walked up to Frank. "I sold the trailer this morning. Pat and I are going out to look at a bungalow in the morning. How about joining us?"

Frank reluctantly agreed.

141

Early the next day, on the way to the bungalow site, the first baseman was plainly boiling inside, and little Andy was the only occupant of the car who did not know why. A column in the *Denver Morning Star* had subtly inferred that steers and horses were not compatible and that it was a crying shame that certain termites were allowed in the ball park. Pat Van Etten managed to get Frank alone for a few moments while Ray inspected the heating plant. Unmistakably distraught, she pleaded with the second baseman to keep a close watch on Ray.

"I'll try," he said, "but it's quite a large order, Pat."

Bert Moger, his rugged face rock-hard, waved a copy of the *Star* at the Denver players when they had all suited up that night. "I know this writer. He does not sound off without good reason. I'm not accusing anyone here, but if I ever catch any man on this club as much as talking to certain shady characters or catch him within three blocks of a joint known as the Blue Rail I'll fine him a month's pay."

Before the Steers vacated the dressing room Frank tried to draw Ray aside, but the first baseman got a few words in first. "How much of me does the club own? What is Moger running, a Boys Town?"

"You go ahead and dump over your applecart, Ray. Don't forget Pat and little Andy will be in it."

"My family is my business, *Uncle* Frank!"

Frank's usually mild eyes smoldered. "I'll remember that, believe me!"

"Frank, I—" The first baseman kicked an empty beverage can the length of the room when the second baseman walked hurriedly out of the dressing room.

During the pre-game infield drill, Frank had the feeling that he was getting caught in the middle again and was about ready to get squeezed. He had to remember

Tom Thorp's warning against forever being a target for imposition. A pawn, he reminded himself, was a chessman of lowest rank, and unless he took himself well in hand he would find himself rooked once more. He fielded a grounder and put all the steam that was in him behind the throw to Van Etten at first, and the bonus player was almost too late getting his glove up. Frank trotted toward Ray. "I'm sorry. I just——"

Van Etten said, "Nuts. You had a right to try and skull me," and he gave the second baseman his back and fired the ball to the plate.

Bert Moger picked Herbie Kamm, a left-hander, to go against the Chicks that night, and the Steers stampeded in the last of the fourth and gave him a five-run bulge, Frank driving in two with a bases-loaded single. Portland began pecking away at Kamm and scored a run in each of the next three innings. They tied it up, 6-6, in the top of the eighth before Moger brought Tim McGinley in from the bullpen. Hack Shellenbach led off when the Steers came in to hit, and Van Etten moved into the on-deck circle. The Chicks on the bench got their beaks into him. "Hey, playboy! Can you get me a date with a bunny tonight? How did you hit 'em at Vegas?"

Van Etten threw a look at the Portland bench and gave them an age-old very impolite gesture that brought a roar of disapproval from the over four thousand fans. Frank glanced at Moger and he could almost hear the grinding of the manager's teeth. Steve Holovak said under his breath, "I smell smoke!"

The crowd screamed for more when Shellenbach sliced a single to the opposite field. Now they were mindful of Van Etten's virtues rather than his sins when he moved in and faced the Chick pitcher. The big right-hander lowered his head to get the sign from his receiver, grinned, and nodded. He cut loose with a fast ball that rocked Van Etten back on his heels. The next pitch sent him sprawling into the dirt, and Bert Moger was out of the dugout even before his first baseman got to his feet, whipped off his hard hat and threw it at the Portland pitcher.

Both benches emptied, and a full-sized riot was forestalled only by a flying tackle on the part of the Chick catcher. Finally cooled off, the Steer first baseman was ordered to the showers, and the fans let him know in full voice that they did not care if he drowned. The umpire laid some letters of baseball law down to the Chick pitcher, then ordered the game to go on.

Frank could not get little Andy Van Etten out of his mind as he abstractedly watched Jimmy Braden take up where Ray had left off. Braden was a left-handed pull-hitter and he had the power to hit it all the way. He took a strike and then swung at a high fast ball and drove it over the barrier in right to put Denver out in front, 8-6. Tim McGinley saw that the score stayed that way, and when the Steers reached the dressing room Ray Van Etten was sitting in front of his locker, somewhat contrite. "Bert," he said to the manager, "That pitcher was trying to skull me. I'm too young to die."

"That's a matter of opinion," Moger snapped back, and a lot of the Steers grinned or laughed outright.

Van Etten said, laughing himself, "I led with my chin that time. Frank, I'm moving into the new house tomorrow and could use a man to help load the U-Haul."

The second baseman nodded. When he reached the apartment a half hour later, both Hack Shellenbach and Nick Saba agreed that he should not get too palsy walsy with the bonus player. "I've been in bridge and gin games with Van Etten, Frank," Hack said. "He plays everything for blood and he'll gamble on anything, even the direction the flags on the ball parks will blow on a certain day. I have a hunch his career will be short and not too sweet."

"He's a big kid not quite grown up," Frank argued. "That bonus money he got didn't help any. I'm sure he'll straighten out."

"Okay, Frank. But remember, we warned you."

On Friday night, Moger presented a lineup at the plate that had Jimmy Braden at first in place of Van Etten. When he returned to the bench he met Van Etten's resentful glance and ground out, "Cool your heels for a while, Ray, and in the process some of the air-conditioning might go to your head."

Karl Braun, Moger's right-hander, got in trouble after the leadoff man had grounded out. A walk and a single to right put Chicks on first and third with one out, but Frank flagged down a grass-cutter far to his right and flipped to Scully, covering second, who fired to Braden for the double play. The crowd gave the second baseman a round of applause when the Steers came off, but Frank was only partly aware of it. He wondered if the Milwaukee front office was aware of his .273 batting average and his minimum of boots in the field.

He was forcefully reminded of the fact that the long ball and runs-batted-in specialist was still the apple of the owner's and scouts' eyes a few minutes later when Mike Gurstine hit for the circuit with two men on. When Mike crossed the plate, the crowd turned loose a deafening roar that lasted for over a minute. Frank went out to wait while Kaula hit, and he had to grope far back to the time he had hit a home run. When Kaula popped up to the Chick infield, he made his way to the plate, the Portland jockeys working on him. One opined that people may have seen a purple cow but never a bowlegged one.

Frank grinned out at the Chick pitcher and choked up

on the bat a little. Already combed for three runs, the right-hander was close to the boiling point and he reared back and shaved Frank close. The second baseman started for first, but the umpire called him back. Bert Moger came out fast, backing up Frank's assertion that the ball had nicked his sleeve. The Steers on the bench took over when the manager walked away—particularly Ray Van Etten—and the man in blue walked halfway to the Denver dugout, stabbing at the Steers with a big index finger. "One more word," he bellowed, "and I'll clear the bench!"

Before he dug in at the plate again Frank saw Moger jawing at Ray, and he was certain the first baseman was building a doghouse for himself, board by board. The next pitch came in just under his letters, and he poked it just as it started to break and dumped it into short left for a single. Steve Holovak, long overdue in the long ball department, tripled down the alley in right and sent Frank across with Denver's fourth run. The Portland pilot hurried out to the hill to change pitchers. The relief man got Nick Saba to fly to right.

It was a night for the Steers to stomp and bellow, and they pounded four Chick pitchers for fourteen runs. In the dressing room Moger even gave Van Etten a grin.

Frank was out at the Van Ettens' the next afternoon tossing a ball across the living room with little Andy when the doorbell rang, and the second baseman wondered why Ray waved Pat off in such a hurry when she was about to answer it. Frank got a glimpse of a man at the door and a big car parked out in front before Ray closed the door again. There was an expression on Ray's face Frank did not exactly like when he waved a long white envelope at his wife. "A guy just paid back a loan I'd nearly forgot," he said. "Now you can get the new dishwasher."

Frank was positive that there was doubt in Pat Van Etten's brown eyes, and that her smile was forced. "I saw the big car drive away, Ray," she said. "Why would a man who owned one like that have to borrow money?"

"Ha, did you know that President Kennedy used to borrow cigar money from the congressmen when he was in the White House?"

Frank cornered Ray out in the back yard and asked the first baseman cold turkey if that had been a bet he'd won. The first baseman did not throw back a curve. "All right, so I bet a guy the Steers would win tonight, and I got three for every two. What's wrong in backing your own club to win?"

"You can ask a couple of pro football players if you ever meet them, Ray," Frank said. "They got suspended for a whole season and were lucky to get back at all. Look, we're supposed to be friends, and people are judged by the close company they keep, Ray. I can't afford to get spattered with——"

"Yeah," Van Etten said coldly. "So go spill it all to Moger."

"You know better than that," Frank said, and forced a grin. "I'd rather fight than snitch. Ray, you're an intelligent man and you must know I'm only interested in your——"

Little Andy came running out of the house loaded down with two gloves, a bat and a catcher's mask. "Le's play ball!" he shouted.

Frank said quickly, "I have to be going. While you're playing with Andy, think of what you might do to him."

The Steers won five out of six in the short home stand, and invaded Salt Lake. Three hours before a twilight game was to start, Van Etten barged into the hotel room and loudly declared open season on the local sports writer, George Barr. "I'll sue this guy for his last pair of shorts!" he vowed, and dropped a copy of the *Salt Lake City Register* in the second baseman's lap. Frank read the story slowly, doubting as he went along that there was any libel involved. Innuendo, however, was rampant.

You would naturally think Bert Moger, with his Steers leading the pack in the league's southern division by three games, would be a most happy man, but if we are to believe our contemporaries the Denver manager is faced with one of those personality problems that crop up in baseball every few years. Ray Van Etten, signed out of college for a big bonus, is hitting close to .380 at the plate and seems to have solved the Denvers' first base deficiency, but the man's apparent scorn for the standard rules of behavior on and off the diamond could well direct him into the unfortunate footsteps of half a dozen ballplayers we could name before him.

Van Etten's unbridled temper has already banished him from two ball games with the season scarcely under way. He has had one fine levied against him and has received stern warnings as to his association with characters who walk the shady side of the street. The man is a paradox. He is trigger-tempered, yet anything but belligerent, and could not be classified as a "showboat." We would say he was a high-strung young man resentful of discipline, one who has the talent to go far if his temperament does not devour those talents . . .

"So he's a head doctor!" Ray fairly shouted. "He'll need one if he doesn't get off my back."

Frank threw the newspaper aside. "Ray, just be thankful that little Andy can't read the newspapers yet. You can't dispute anything Barr said in that story. You've been seen back in Denver with Vinnie Disko. Nearly five thousand fans saw you talking with him in the ball park.

When people see and smell smoke they soon holler 'Fire!' "

"I don't drink, Frank, and only once in a while I smoke a pipe. I married the only girl I ever wanted, so haven't I got a right to one small vice, if you call betting on something once in a while just that?"

"Baseball was nearly ruined once by gamblers, Ray. They just can't let it happen again. Let just one horse bet or a single I.O.U. come out in the open and you're dead. You are a ballplayer and you're public domain. Ballplayers generally make the brickbats or the bouquets the writers throw at them."

Van Etten gave Frank a small grin. "When I want your opinion, knucklehead, I'll tell you."

● FOURTEEN

A FEW DAYS LATER IN OKLAHOMA CITY, WHILE BERT
Moger made a pitching change in the fifth inning of a
twilight game, Ray left the first sack and walked over to
Frank. "This'll be over before nine o'clock," he said. "I
got a call from a guy I knew at college this morning. His
old man is loaded and likes to be seen with ballplayers.
Want to do the town tonight—up to midnight?"

"Not interested," the second baseman said, watching
Tim McGinley throw his warmups. "I'm just a country
kid, remember?" He grinned behind his glove. "You ask
Bert Moger?"

"You are a riot," Van Etten snapped. "The next
roomie I get on the road won't be one who's taken the
vows." He went back to his position when the Oiler hitter
stepped up to the plate and waved his bat at McGinley.
Herbie Kamm had left runners on second and third with

only one out. The veteran reliefer got the batter to slam a grounder at Phil Scully, and the shortstop held the runners on and fired to Van Etten for the second out. Frank leaped high to haul down a screaming liner that seemed labeled for at least two bases, to get the Steers out of the inning and still leading, 5-4.

McGinley went all the way, to nail down a 7-4 win for Denver, and Bert Moger, smacking his lips over a five-game winning streak, had a grin for everybody in the visitors' dressing room. "I'll bet he won't make a bed check tonight," Van Etten said to Frank before going into the shower. You changed your mind about——?"

Frank shook his head. "I wish you would, Ray."

"So I'm going out to have a little fun. I'll get loaded with ginger ale and maybe see a couple of pretty night club entertainers," the first baseman said, shaking his head. "That's terrible? Frank, I've seen squares, but you take the blue ribbon."

It was well after midnight when the light in the hotel room was snapped on and roused Frank out of fitful sleep. After he shook the cobwebs out of his head, one glance at Ray convinced him that the first baseman was anything but enchanted over his night out. "Well, how did it go?" he asked, and sat up in bed.

Van Etten fired his summer jacket across the room. "It started out fine," he said. "We went to a place called Avant Garde. Then one of those dames with a camera took a picture, and I made it clear to her that I wasn't having any. Some guy got nasty with me and I had to push him back in his chair. Paul Weckman's old man is a regular customer there and he saw to it that the negative wouldn't be printed. We left there and went to another place for a while. When I got back to the hotel, there was

Mike Greer, Moger's bird dog, sitting in the lobby. 'It'll most likely cost you another twenty-five,' he says to me."

"You're no shrinking violet, Ray. Why the beef about the picture?"

"Paul had a blonde with him. When she saw the camera trained on us she put an arm around me. If Pat ever——"

"Yeah," Frank said, and slid back under the covers. If he had any sense at all, he told himself, he would see the road secretary after breakfast and demand a switch in roomies. A man was generally judged by the company he kept. But there was little Andy and a promise he had made to the boy's mother, and a small grin swept over his face as he fell asleep. Who but a second baseman could be expected to be caught in the middle?

The writing fraternity, especially those members specializing in the game of baseball, are unbelievably quick in pouncing upon off-the-diamond copy, and the Oklahoma scribes took liberties with the mild hassle in the Avant Garde. But for the intervention of a certain man of wealth and influence, they intimated, the Denver first baseman could easily have started a riot. A patron was considering an assault charge against Van Etten, and Bert Moger, the manager of the Steers, would most certainly take a dim view of the bonus player's latest escapade and act accordingly.

Van Etten was summoned to Moger's room after the manager read the morning paper. Returning a half hour later, he told Frank, "He hit me for fifty dollars this time, mostly for breaking the curfew. He said the next time he had to call me on the carpet would mean a three-day suspension. I asked him what Jimmy Braden was hitting. I told him I would not mind being traded."

"Sure, you're hitting about three-sixty," Frank said,

"but don't let it go to your head. The pitching gets better as the season goes along and it is easy to drop fifty points in a couple of weeks. Get something through your thick skull, Ray. Moger would swap a headache for a two-eighty hitter in a minute."

"Want to bet on that?"

"I'm tempted to," the second baseman said impatiently. "Your coat came back from the tailor shop while you were gone, along with a handicapping sheet they found in the pocket. Man, if Moger ever found that in a locker room!"

"I'd take the fifth amendment," the first baseman said, his grin exasperating.

Frank slipped on his coat and headed for the door. "I need some aspirin," he threw over his shoulder.

The Steer first baseman, when he stepped in to hit in the last of the second inning that night, got the jumbo-sized going-over from the Oiler bench jockeys. They wanted the platinum blonde's telephone number. When he swung at a pitch and missed, one stout-lunged Oiler yelled, "Those flash bulbs are bad for the old peepers, playboy!"

The fans joined in with their own particular brand of abuse, and he stepped out and got dirt on his hands. He took a ball, fouled a pitch off, then went over to the on-deck circle for the pine tar rag. An Oiler shouted, "Give him a bar rag, Mike," and Gurstine, the next Denver hitter, had to laugh, himself. Leaning against the bat rack, Frank thought for a long moment that the first baseman would make Mike swallow the sticky rag, and then he let his pent-up breath escape when Van Etten strode back to the plate. The first baseman fanned, kicked up some dirt, and walked away.

Mike Gurstine ripped a double to right, scoring Phil

Scully who had walked and stole second, and Frank went out there to wait behind Sid Kaula. The catcher skied to left, and Joe Plachette, Moger's right-hander, made his way to the mound. He carried the slim 1-0 lead into the sixth, then got into trouble. Four hits and two runs later, he tossed the ball to relief pitcher Bill Mooring, leaving Oilers on first and second. The Oklahoma catcher, with one out, worked the string out, then blooped a fly into short right that seemed certain to drop in, but Frank ran back at full speed, yelled the right fielder off, and lunged at the ball as it dropped toward the grass a few feet ahead of him. He caught it inches from the ground, turned a somersault, and heard Holovak yell at him. He flipped it to the right fielder, who fired to first to nail the Oiler runner trying to get back there.

The partisan crowd gave him a round of applause as he trotted in, and he wondered if any of the Milwaukee scouts happened to be in town. The hit he'd made in the second inning, the walk he'd drawn in the fifth, had upped his batting average to .272. This might mean *the* year. He was in his prime and he knew it. He'd never be better than he was at this very minute, and any kind of a setback could well prove disastrous.

The score was still 2-1 in favor of the Oilers when the Steers came in to hit in the first of the ninth. Moger sent in a pinch hitter to bat for Plachette, and the utility out-fielder reached first on a boot by the Oklahoma third base-man. Phil Scully fouled out, and Shellenbach shortened up and laid down a perfect bunt, putting the tieing run on second. Moger called Van Etten back and gave Jimmy Braden the nod. "Bring the run in," the manager said, and then turned to meet Van Etten's stormy glance. "They've given you rabbit ears out there," he said, "and you didn't know whether you were swinging a bat or a tennis racket. And bear in mind that you were warned."

Frank grabbed Ray by the arm when it seemed that the bonus player was about to lose control. "Sit down, Ray," he cautioned. "Knock it off."

Braden took two pitches wide of the plate, fouled off a curve, then smashed the clutch hit into left to tie up the ball game. Mike Gurstine, one pitch later, tripled to deep right center to drive the pinch hitter in and give the Steers a 3-2 lead. Kaula couldn't keep it going and Denver took the field with Braden at first and Tim McGinley, the workhorse, on the mound. The veteran fireman refused the Oilers even the start of a small blaze, and the Steers took their sixth straight win to the dressing room.

Under the shower Frank thought of Tom Thorp's philosophy and knew he should wash Ray out of his hair and give up being a restraining influence—for day by day, from one month to the next, a ballplayer faced that inexorable "now or never." He knew that five years in baseball was comparable to fifteen or twenty in the business world outside. Hundreds of ballplayers before him had known the point of no return. For most men the road up from the low bushes was all uphill; the way back was as steep as a toboggan slide. He would have a talk with Bert Moger before noon tomorrow.

At the hotel, Ray Van Etten put in a call to Denver. Listening to the man talk to his wife and small son, Frank knew he would leave things as they were. The first baseman turned a glance his way. "Little Andy wants to say hello, Frank."

He talked to the youngster for a few moments, until Pat Van Etten took over. "Frank," she said, "I read something in tonight's paper. About——"

"It was nothing, believe me. They made a lot out of nothing at all, Pat. He's hot copy and——"

"Keep him down, Frank, please. Sit on him."

"A big order, but I'll try."

He handed Ray the phone, wondering what that thing they called "the whammy" looked like—that hand of fate that sank its claws into *willing* victims. Whatever its guise, he had the feeling that it was lying in ambush for him again, somewhere along the road ahead.

The Steers' streak was broken in Fort Worth, and they managed no more than five hundred ball during the next two weeks, Van Etten and Mike Gurstine both trying to get out of slumps. The first baseman had declared war on the fans all over the circuit, and in Portland he had tried to invade the front seats back of first with a baseball bat. George Barr, the *Salt Lake City Register* sports writer, welcomed the Denver club to town with one of his choicest stints. And when Ray Van Etten read it, Frank could hear the man's blood boiling.

Bert Moger's Denver Steers arrive today to open a three game series with the Bees. Local fans will get another good look at the playboy of the western baseball world, and we mean none other than that living example of why big bonuses should not be paid to ballplayers, Ray Van Etten. We doubt a rumor to the effect that Bee owner Harry Kittrell has requested help from the National Guard during this series with the Bees.

Van Etten, his batting average steadily shrinking, has been a juicy target for the fans from Hawaii to San Diego, and at the moment is suffering from an acute case of rabbit ears. His favorite tunes are "Curfew shall not ring tonight," and "Pony boy." It is this writer's opinion that Jimmy Braden will be Moger's regular first baseman by the time this pennant race reaches the halfway mark. That Van Etten's intractability has contributed to the Steers' slide into second

156

place in the eastern division of the league can scarcely be denied, and his influence over an important cog in Moger's infield is a source of more than mild conjecture among the Steer players. Reverting to the subject of the paying of unreasonable bonuses to . . .

Van Etten threw the paper to the floor, then kicked it in several sections across the room. "I'll go over there and put his head in his lap," he raged. "I'll give him a dentist's bill that will take three years to pay!"

"Ray, I'll bet he's sorry he wrote that right this minute," Frank said. "You've heard about his weakness —that he seldom writes a word without a bottle at his elbow."

"That underhanded crack he made about you! You going to take it without——?"

"I'm ignoring it, Ray."

Van Etten snorted his impatience, went to the phone and called the newspaper. He asked for George Barr, was told the man was not in but got his home number, and in a few moments he made contact with the scribe and unloaded. "Barr? This is Ray Van Etten. This time you got too personal in your lousy column. I'm clipping it, and then I am cramming it down your throat the first time I run into you!" He slammed the phone back on its cradle without waiting for Barr's reaction. "Two will get you five he'll run scared while we're in town."

Frank did not agree. "Sports writers have to save face, Ray, like umpires. Get a couple of hits tonight and you'll forget all about it."

Suiting up for the twilight game late that afternoon, Frank kept praying that Barr would not come into the dressing room, and his prayers were answered. Ray said, as they walked out into the crowd's building racket, "What did I tell you?"

"Lay off, Ray. Just keep your mind working on how to

get out of the slump. Look who's throwing for the Bees tonight. Sad Sam Jamison."

After Phil Scully struck out, the Denver first baseman went out to wait in the on-deck station behind Hack Shellenbach, and the crowd began working on him. The Bees on the bench jabbed him unmercifully with their stingers. Sad Sam, his fast ball buzzing, threw a third strike by Shellenbach, and then the derisive roar boiled out of the seats when Ray Van Etten stepped in. Frank, fighting off a sense of deep foreboding, called for help from on high once more, asking that Ray get himself a hit. Jamison, a dusky southpaw with a toothpaste ad smile, had ambitions of his own, and he got the Steer first baseman to pop up to the infield on a two and two pitch.

The Bees made honey against Leo Bourk in the bottom of the first, scoring two runs, and only a diving catch on Frank's part saved the Steer pitcher from an early shower. Moger gave him a pat on the rear when he came into the visitors' dugout. "Keep it up, Frank," the manager said under his breath. "It should be Duhamel's last good year at Milwaukee."

"You tell *him*," the second baseman said, forcing a grin.

In the top of the fourth, with Shellenbach on first via the hard way, hit by a pitch, Van Etten, belabored by the fans, ran the count full, then lined to the Bee shortstop. Mike Gurstine, long overdue, took a strike, two balls, another strike, then stunned the heckling crowd with a drive that cleared the ball park. It was the impetus Moger's hitters needed, and Kaula followed up with a ringing single to right. Frank dug in against Sad Sam, and a stout-lunged Bee benchman yelled, "Do you press Van Etten's pants?"

A little shaken, Frank let Jamison's first pitch go by for a strike. He swung at a slider and fouled it into the seats back of third. The Salt Lake City bench jockey kept hammering at him. "You belong to the bookie-of-the-month club, too, Hyatt?" Frank stepped out and got dirt on his hands. Back in, he waited Jamison out, and with the count two balls and two strikes he chopped at a half-speed curve and popped a fly into short right just inside the foul line that eluded both the Bee first baseman and right fielder, and Kaula sprinted to third. Mike Holovak skied deep to center, the third run scoring for the Steers. When Nick Saba struck out, Moger made a change in his infield. He put Jimmy Braden on first.

Out at second, Frank involuntarily flashed a look at the press section, and he wished the man would be called out of town for some good reason or another before the game was over. Moger's move had without a doubt shortened Ray's time fuse. He got his mind to leave Barr alone and dwell upon Richard Duhamel, Milwaukee's second baseman. They were saying Richie's legs were beginning to go, and it was a fact that he was hitting only .247. So next year, perhaps . . . It had better be, Frank grimly mused, as he shifted a little to his right to guard against the Bee pull-hitter first up against Bourk.

The game went eleven innings, and the crowd was limp when Steve Holovak drove Frank in from second after two were out. Tim McGinley stopped the Bees in the bottom of the eleventh, and Denver moved off with a 7-6 win. The Steers found Van Etten still in the dressing room stretched out on a bench, and a lot of eyebrows lifted. The first baseman sat up, grinned coldly, and said, "I've been expecting a visitor, but I guess he chickened out."

Moger seldom missed a stick of sports copy, on or off the road. "Start anything with the man and you're a dead duck, understand?"

"How much do you expect me to take, Bert?"

"All you ask for," Moger ground out, "which is plenty, including a Milwaukee reform school like Davenport or Grand Forks."

There was a sense of humor in the first baseman, usually dormant. "They wouldn't dare!" he said with a grin.

Frank lost no time peeling off his flannels and getting under the shower, for he wanted Ray out of there lest Barr crash in the dressing room and loudly call the first baseman's bluff. The gleam of anticipation in the eyes of the other Steer players had not been lost on him. Finally dressed for the street, he hustled his roomie out to the bus that waited to take the Denver club to the hotel. "I knew that guy would crawl," Ray said. "I'll let any other writer quote me."

"You do that, rockhead," Frank said, "and when you're riding those buses out on the prairies you'll wish you used the brains you were born with. Leave it alone, Ray. Let it drop!"

● FIFTEEN

EVERYTHING SEEMED UNDER CONTROL ABOUT AN HOUR later when Frank wrote the last paragraph of a letter home. Ray, clad only in shorts and apparently in for the night, was stretched out on his bed reading a paperback novel. "Reading some of this stuff about Cuba burns me," he suddenly said. "I would have dropped a bomb right in Fidel's lap before he brought the Reds in, if I'd been President."

"I believe it," the second baseman said, and grinned at Van Etten. "Let's hope that if a Van Etten ever becomes President his first name'll be Andy. You have any stamps, Ray?"

The first baseman shook his head, and Frank reached for his jacket. "Anything you want downstairs?"

Van Etten shook his head and went back to his reading.

Down in the lobby a few minutes later, Frank was turning away from the newsstand when he saw George Barr heading for the elevators, and the writer's gait seemed a little unsteady. He hurried across the lobby and caught up with Barr just before the elevator door slid shut. The man's breath was strong and his eyes were red-rimmed. "That big loud mouth up in his room, Hyatt?"

"Look, Barr, you've had one too many," Frank said. "We don't want any trouble with you. Why don't you just go home and forget about it?"

"Let him get me laughed out of town? I'm going to give him what he asked for in spades, Hyatt, and you keep out of my way."

"You haven't a chance with him, Barr. Be a nice guy and——"

"Mind your cotton pickin' business, Hyatt!" the sports writer said, his eyes ablaze. The elevator stopped at the tenth floor and the door automatically opened. Barr said under his breath, "It's room ten-twelve, right? You keep out of my way, Buster, or Moger'll have two ballplayers out of action!" He nearly shoved Frank off his feet when they were clear of the elevator and the second baseman's even temper became a little lopsided.

"Watch it, Barr!" he warned. "I'm telling you, this is as far as you go!"

"You kiddin'?" Barr blurted out, his face flaming red. "I'll get me a piece of Van Etten if I have to walk over you and the whole Denver ball club!" He swung a fist that caught Frank in the left shoulder and sent him against the wall, and the second baseman's only thought as he bounced off was the possibility of an injury that could ruin all the years he had left. He met Barr's rush with an uppercut that sent the writer staggering back-wards along the corridor, and doors began to open on the tenth floor when Barr regained his balance and charged Frank like a wild steer. Blood trickled from the writer's mouth as Frank evaded a wild swing and got his arms around the man and wrestled him to the carpet. The second baseman felt hands pulling at him, heard voices the length of the corridor.

He shoved Barr away from him and then got up and looked around him at the faces of Shellenbach, Mike Gurstine, Phil Scully and Ray Van Etten. Four other players soon arrived on the scene, along with Bert Moger, clad in pajamas and dressing gown.

"Frank," Ray choked out, "you——?"

Barr got to his feet, shocked cold sober, and drew the back of a hand across his bleeding mouth. He laid a flat glance against Moger. "I came here to have a talk with Van Etten, but this guy jumped me, Bert. M-Maybe I was to blame—in a way. I——"

"He came looking for trouble," Frank said in defense. "He had a little too much to drink. He threw the first punch, and I doubt if I can swing a bat for a couple of days."

Moger said, "Get out of here, Barr!" Half a dozen curious guests had appeared. He eyed Van Etten askance before chasing the ballplayers back to their rooms. "I have no doubt you invited him here, in your own friendly way, and Hyatt gets the dirty end of it. Somebody has to take the rap for this and it won't be the press. Van Etten, you're as bad as a typhoid carrier. All right, break it up!"

"I'm sorry, Frank," the first baseman said when they reached their room. "Couldn't you have stopped Barr without——?"

"He was out to murder me, and all I could think of was a broken hand or some busted ribs," the second baseman said, half sick with the thought of what all this would do to him. He gave Van Etten a twisted smile. "If he'd gotten to you before I—well, I thought of that before he slugged me. I didn't have a wife and kid and—" He smashed a fist down against a pillow. "Just call me the world's prize sucker!"

"Frank, I am really sorry. What more can I say? Look, you've never been one half-step out of line before, and it was self defense."

"No witnesses, Ray. Barr has to think of his job, too, and don't forget he took a dig at me in that story. Have you forgotten about that pitcher with the Angels who got exiled to the minors? It happened almost like this! Right now, Ray, I'm so scared I could throw up. I figured this year I'd have a good chance of making it to the big leagues, but——"

"You're building this thing up out of all proportion," Van Etten said. "In the morning it'll have shrunk down to its proper size. And I'll bet you half a month's pay that Barr will go to bat for you."

"Oh, sure," the second baseman said dismally, "and the Washington Solons will win the American League pennant."

Disciplinarian action, in view of Frank Hyatt's previous record of exemplary behavior—a ten-day suspension and a hundred dollar fine—was not too severe in itself, but heartbreaking developments followed. Bert Moger put a nineteen-year-old kid named Lenny Ripon at second base in the second tilt with the Bees and he banged out three hits. During the next ten days he hit for a .301 average, and when the next long road trip began Frank found himself glued to the bench when Moger was in no need for a runner or a pinch hitter. When the Steers opened a three game series in Tacoma, Ray Van Etten's hold on the first base job was in jeopardy. His batting average was far below .300, his patience with umpires almost zero."

"Get going, Ray," Frank said when the first baseman went up to hit in the top of the first. He knew the man was pressing too hard and suffering from a guilt complex since the incident in Salt Lake City, and everywhere they had been riding him hard. Van Etten went out there and popped up, and then fired his bat and hard hat toward the Steer bench.

The fans roundly booed him, and when the first baseman reached the dugout Moger snapped, "You can take the rest of the night off, Ray!"

Frank sat back, in his mind reading over the letter that he had received from Tom Thorp following his suspension, and admitted that he deserved every scathing line of it. He had let himself be used from the time he was born and if he ever became his own man he would be tripping over a long white beard. He had no better than Class AA gumption and some day perhaps he could buy a ticket into a Big League park.

He watched Lenny Ripon single a run home in the top of the second, and overrun the keystone sack when Steve Holovak singled into right. A good throw cut him down. With the score even at 2-2 going into the seventh, Jimmy Braden doubled with the bases jammed and put the Steers in front, 4-2. Herbie Kamm had all his good stuff the rest of the way and left the mound with his ninth win of the year. Frank shed an almost spotless road uniform in the visitors' side of the dressing room and took his time showering. He sat on the long bench, his eyes on Lenny Ripon, envying the teen-ager's youth and spirit, and wondered if he had really lost both. He finally washed off, and was dressing when Bert Moger came up and said, "Don't let it get you down, Frank. The kid's bat is hot, but I have a hunch the pitchers will get him the next time around."

The manager's prediction proved correct, and when Lenny Ripon's bat failed to compensate for only adequate fielding, Frank found himself at the old stand when the Steers opened a home set with the Oklahoma Oilers. When he came to bat for the first time in the last of the second, with Mike Gurstine leading off first, a smattering of fans chose to rib rather than join in the round of applause. The Oilers on the bench cooperated fully. They wanted to know if it had been a sports writer who had knocked him bowlegged. How much was he getting as a bodyguard for Van Etten? "He-e-e-e-e-ey, sorehead!"

After fouling a pitch off, then missing one by a foot, he knew his timing was off. A change-up fooled him completely and he took the third strike with his bat on his shoulder. The layoff, he discovered a few minutes later, had not affected his play in the field, but it gave him small consolation. There was already a surplus of "good field, no hit" in the majors.

Plachette, working for the Steers, lost his control in the sixth. With two on, the Oiler catcher, Nedick, tripled over Mike Gurstine's head in center, and when Plachette walked the next hitter, Moger came out with the hook. Before the fire was put out, the visitors had four runs. Frank came up to hit in the Denver half with Jimmy Braden on third and just one out, and swung at a one and two pitch. He hit a comebacker to the Oiler pitcher, giving him nothing for three for the night. He had another chance to drive in a run in the eighth, but hit a soft liner into the Oklahoma City shortstop's hands. The Steers lost it, 5-4, leaving two runners on in the last of the ninth, and Frank, on the way to the dressing room, wished a man's life, like the pages of a book, could be turned back. A personality change at the right time might come in handy, too. He was, he told himself, quoting a famous comic strip character, just what he was and that's all he could be.

After breakfast the next morning a phone call from the Van Etten home turned his cereal a little sour in his stomach. "Moger called me a few minutes ago," Ray said, his voice a little reedy. "I'm being sent down to Austin. Know anybody wants to buy a house?"

Frank, struck dumb for a few moments, finally managed to say, "I certainly never expected it. How's Pat taking it?"

"In stride, Frank. In fact, she figures it's the best thing that ever happened to me." He forced a laugh. "What is it they call it—youthful offender treatment? I'm to take off in the morning, so come on out and have a good cry with me."

There was not a sign of gloom in the Van Etten menage when the second baseman arrived. "I asked for it, Frank," Ray said, "because I had a big fat head and a bigger mouth, and I just couldn't take prosperity. What Pat told me is right—I nearly dragged you down with me. I want you to know I appreciate all you tried to do for me."

"You'll be back before you know it, Ray. Most likely you'll jump right into the majors."

"I intend to do just that. Pat and Little Andy will be around for a while until this house is sold, so look in on them once in a while, Frank."

When he left, he carried a gift from Andy, a crude drawing of a ballplayer reaching for a high one. It was signed with a laborious scrawl, "To Uncle Frank—from his pal, Andy." He had felt like taking the little guy aside to tell him that he shouldn't get too soft in this rugged

167

world or he would find himself behind the eight ball—
that he would find himself being used like a pawn on a
chessboard. Instead, he had said, "I'll be seeing you,
sport. You eat your wheatniks every morning."

Three weeks later he was still struggling to get his
batting mark over .260, and it was not until the season
was three-quarters over that he finally began to get his
share of hits. Major league clubs began reaching for
pennant-stretch strength, and the Philly Quakers got
Mike Gurstine in a deal with the Milwaukee front office.
Leo Bourk was the key man in a three-player transaction
with the Detroit Panthers, and the Steers, when they
moved into San Diego for a twi-night doubleheader, had
three new players suiting up.

Swallowing bitter disappointment, Frank stiffened his
upper lip and vented his spleen on Coast League pitching, punching out three hits, one a double, against San
Diego hurling in the twilight affair. He got two for three
in the nightcap, and when he stripped off in the dressing
room, Moger said, "What kept you, Frank?"

"My lovable disposition," the second baseman said, his
grin saturine. "Isn't that why you don't want to lose me,
Bert?"

The manager said, "Drop into my room before you hit
the sack tonight, Frank."

It was close to midnight when he was told that Detroit
had mentioned him in the deal for Leo Bourk. "They
didn't want to give us enough cash or the player we figured was full value received," Moger revealed. "Like I've
said before, the Chiefs know Richie Duhamel has seen all
his best years and they have to have insurance. So drown
your sorrows, Frank, and keep getting your base hits."

Frank said, "You make it sound terrific, Bert. So while
I'm waiting, some hot shot off a campus, a Joe College

like Ray Van Etten, will knock my spikes from under me. The youth kick is everywhere."

"Well, I've told you. Now get out of here and let me get some sleep."

The Denver second baseman finished the season with a .272 batting average, found himself still at second for Denver when the spring training season opened in Waycross, Georgia, and was about ready to completely resign himself to Triple A ball in late August of the same year, despite his .278 average at the plate. And then came that glorious evening when Bert Moger took him aside and told him he was to report to the Milwaukee Chiefs within forty-eight hours. . . .

<hr>

Again he shook himself loose from the past, and he needed a few seconds to become fully aware of where he really was—in the Milwaukee dressing room amid last-minute confusion, with Joe Arriga, Al Jansky, and Ira Eckert, and all the others. Hy Brown said, "All right, Frank, let's go, and good luck out there."

He was in the dugout looking out at the big crowd in the County Stadium when he heard of the last-minute changes Sam Kelso had made in his lineup. Vanderpool would start in place of Duhamel, and a Negro southpaw, Jason Bozer, brought up in a recent deal with the Redlegs from Wichita, would throw against the Metros. When the Chiefs took the field, Pete Ibarra, sensing Frank's impatience and resentment, said through his big quid of scrap tobacco, "Keep your shirt on, kid. Remind me to show you the callouses I've got under me while waiting to strike out. Sittin' here, you can't do much wrong."

He could have told the veteran how wrong he was,

that he had been struck out more than once far away from a ball park because of his vulnerability to imposition. But he kept silent and watched the Metro leadoff hitter ground out to Johnny Drew at third. Bozer got the next batter into a two and nothing hole, then broke off a curve that sent the Metro hitter back to the dugout with his mouth hanging open. A few moments later Vanderpool, having to go far to his right, bobbled what should have been the third out, and Frank heard a grunt of disapproval from Kelso. The crowd began to come alive when Krist, New York's heavy lumberman, stepped in to hit. The Chiefs in the outfield backtracked, and Al Jansky went out to the mound to make sure the rookie would keep his pitches low and on the outside corner.

Bozer took his time. He threw over to Eckert, but the runner got back. The fans and the Metro bench worked him over when he picked up the rosin bag, and in the glare of the light towers his dark skin glistened with sweat. Krist fouled his first pitch back and over the roof of the stands. The slugger let two wide ones alone, then connected solidly with Bozer's one and two delivery and put it into the right field seats. The Metros' left fielder, Chagares, his batting mark not too far below .300, dug in. Bozer turned and looked at the activity in the Chief bullpen, then went to work again. The inconstant fans howled their approval when he struck Chagares out.

Kelso greeted his rookie pitcher with a broad grin and a slap on the back. "You live and learn, kid. You won't throw that one to Krist again."

"It was like bein' on the high divin' board for the first time." The pitcher grinned. "I'll be okay now, Skipper."

"And when some go down they don't come back up," Frank observed, and was immediately sorry he had betrayed his mood.

Kelso said with a touch of sarcasm, "You think you can hit that Metro southpaw as well as you hit that writer out in Salt Lake City, Hyatt?"

"Touché, Bert," the second baseman said, and joined in with the laughter that rolled the length of the bench.

"Just sit tight, Frank," the manager advised. "You weren't hired for your Barrymore profile."

Hightman, the Metro southpaw, disposed of Provost and Drew with ease, but Raneri rocked him for a double to the left field corner. Joe Arriga was given a free pass when the count ran to three and one, but Hightman quieted the fans by slipping a third strike past Al Jansky. As the Chiefs took the field a horn sounded in the stands, and it sent Frank to wondering if he shouldn't have sounded his a little more on the way up.

His mind started throwing him curves as he watched Bozer work against the Metro hitters. Had George Barr, a convincing talker, worked on Sam Kelso, the scouts, and at least one understanding and sympathetic soul in the Milwaukee front office to bring him to the Big Leagues for only a little while? They could easily lose him in the shuffle during winter trading. He grinned on only one side of his face when he thought of his old teammate at Grand Forks, Duke Lubell, and the man's words were plain in his ears again. "They'll deal out the honor cards, Frank, and discard the rest."

Maybe, he mused, he should have quit that day along with Duke.

SIXTEEN

THE METROS' SHORTSTOP, A FAST MAN, DRAGGED A BUNT, and Bozer raced to his left and collided with Vanderpool charging in. There was no play, and the crowd began squirming. Hy Brown, sitting beside Frank, muttered, "Bozer could've got that guy out. The big kid's too eager."

Richie Duhamel shook his head. "I'd swap one of my ears for his legs. You know somethin'? Why don't ballplayers learn to walk on their hands during the off-seasons?"

The base runner took off when Bozer threw a two and two pitch to the New York hitter, and Jansky fired straight and true to Vanderpool, but the prize rookie let the ball squirt away from him and go into center field. The Metro runner wheeled around to third, and the fans ordered Big Chief Kelso to take Vanderpool's scalp.

On the mound Bozer drew in a deep breath, then leaned forward to get Jansky's sign. He reared back and blazed a third strike by the Metro hitter, and Pete Ibarra, coming away from the fountain, said, "Two sacks of Brown Mule he'll get out of the inning!"

Bozer kept his second pitch too high to the next batter and it was belted deep to left, and the runner on third came in on the sacrifice, but Provost appealed to the umpire at third. His claim that the Metro runner had failed to tag up was sustained, and a rhubarb exploded. The aged Metro skipper charged out of his dugout to back up his raging shortstop and his protesting third base coach. Above the gleeful roar in the stands came derisive sour notes from that horn that Frank felt was directed toward him alone, to remind him that he had been born to step aside and let the parade go by. The umpire out there looked a lot like his brother, Ben.

A montage built up before his mind's eye, blotting out the crowd, and familiar faces took shape; Ben, Duke Lubell, Fred Veck, Cass Rettinger, Ray Van Etten, and Bert Moger, and all of these men had used him in one way or another to their advantage even though they hadn't been exactly aware of it. He grinned as he blinked the vision away. He should have been born during the days of the Congress shoe and the bustle, when men signed themselves, "Yr obedient servant." It was not too late for the worm to turn, he told himself.

Peace was restored in the stadium and Bozer rubbed up a new ball. The Negro southpaw hummed two strikes across the plate, the batter watching them go by, and then he caught the inside corner with a curve that had the Metro leaning back, and Kelso said to his bench as Bozer walked in, "I think we've got something here."

Jason Bozer, reaching the dugout, glared at Pete

173

Ibarra. "That's where I sit, man. My lucky seat, y' hear?"

Ibarra moved, a grin on his face. "Sure, thing, Jase. I beg your pardon."

Frank stared at the southpaw with admiration, marveling at how easy it really was for a man to assert himself, even for a man representing a group that could generally expect some sort of reprisal, and he felt as if he had just taken a shot of adrenalin. The confines of the stadium suddenly seemed to shrink in size, along with the major leaguers at work here. It was not too late to pick up a few loose ends like the money he had loaned Ben, and he'd get it or take it out of the man's hide. He grinned down at the concrete, wishing there were a mirror there so that he might see his new image. He had come into baseball like a lamb and he vowed to go out like a lion.

Ira Eckert led off for Milwaukee and belted a nothing and two pitch past short for a single, and the fans yelled for Martsell to keep things alive. The right fielder looped a Texas Leaguer into short left, and the noise in the stadium built up as Vanderpool stepped in to hit. Frank caught himself yelling at the bonus player along with the other Chiefs and quickly drew back into his new shell. They'd paid that kid out there thousands of dollars worth of encouragement already, so let him produce on his own.

Hightman checked the runners, then began working on the Milwaukee second baseman. He missed with a slider, got his fast ball past Vanderpool for a strike, then brushed the hitter back with another blazer. The rookie seemed shaken up when he stepped out to pick up some dirt, and when he backed away from the plate just as Hightman got ready to throw, Frank was sure the Metro pitcher had the guy in his pocket. He threw a glance at Kelso when Vanderpool slashed at the pitch and hit into an easy double play, but the manager, his hands thrust into the back pockets of his uniform pants, seemed unconcerned.

With Eckert on third and two out, Bozer went down swinging, and the fans subsided and sat on their hands once more.

Frank said under his breath when the working Chiefs cleared the bench, "How long will they go with the rookie?"

Hy Brown flashed him an amused glance. "I buy a big Cadillac, say. I find there's a couple of bugs in it, Frank, so do I turn it in before I take some time working 'em out?"

The utility infielder grinned out at the action. Sure, he was the used jalopy the Chiefs had picked up in case the big, shiny heap blew a gasket. Would they renew the registration on him come another season or dump him back into the minors?

The Metros, enjoying the tag end of the pennant chase as "spoilers," nicked Bozer for another run in the top of the third, their prime pest, Krist, knocking it in. Leading, 3-0, the Metro pitcher seemed to get tougher. He mowed down Provost, Drew, and Raneri in order, and as his team went out there Kelso shouted after them, "Next time try and stay a little longer!"

Frank, after watching the first Metro hitter work Bozer for a walk, got up and moved to the drinking fountain to get water he did not really need. Glued to the bench a ballplayer gets too much time for thinking and is haunted by things he has read in the sports columns. Only yesterday in the *Milwaukee Star* a writer had said that the word was going around the circuit that many a veteran was going to get his pink slip come fall. The trend was to go with youth, and Double and Triple A fans would get a chance to say hello to old favorites on the way down.

When the next batter singled off Drew's glove at third, Sam Kelso went to the top step and waved to his bullpen. Bozer looked in at him, grinned, and waved him back with his glove. He went back to work, got the hitter into a two and nothing hole, then induced him to hit a one-hopper to Provost. Vanderpool took the quick throw from the shortstop, stepped on second and rifled to Eckert, and Bozer grinned toward the dugout. Kelso turned toward the Chiefs' trainer. "I think we'll keep that boy, Tom."

Shugrue said, "They'll never forgive the brass here out at Wichita."

Frank involuntarily nodded his head. A couple of paragraphs he had read in a national magazine came back to him. Why was minor league ball threatened with extinction in most parts of the country? One reason was that Big League clubs called up good minor league players when they actually had no need of them, and they more often than not either rotted away in the bullpen or lost their batting eye languishing on a bench. Minor league cities had lost pennants because of the big late-summer grabs by parent clubs.

The crowd's sudden roar lifted Frank's head up and he saw Eckert camping under a high pop-up that would be the third out. When the colored pitcher came in he asked the Chiefs to get him some runs. "You get me four and we win," he said.

Joe Arriga gave it a big try but missed a home run by a few feet, the New York right fielder hauling his drive down deep on the warning track. Hightman, his aplomb ruffled, worked too carefully on Jansky and lost him, and the fans loudly put it up to Ira Eckert. The first baseman got a green light when he ran the Metro pitcher into the three and one hole and lined a hit to right, Jansky wheeling around to third. Frank threw an anxious look at Kelso when Vanderpool went out to wait behind Martsell. Again the manager seemed willing to stand pat.

Hightman, after a conference with his catcher, slipped two strikes by the Milwaukee right fielder, but Martsell lifted the third pitch to deep left, Jansky scoring the home club's first run. Boos were plentiful when the bonus player took his odd stance at the plate, and for a few unguarded moments Frank felt deep sympathy for the youngster and wished he would break the ice. Hightman got the hitter to swing at a bad pitch, inside, hung up a second strike with a slider that nipped the outside corner, then wasted one. Vanderpool swung at an off-speed curve and fouled out to the New York catcher. As the second baseman threw his protective helmet away, Frank heard Kelso growl under his breath to Ibarra, "Somebody guessed wrong."

The game went into the sixth, the cellar champions still out in front, 3-1. Bozer, appearing to get stronger with each pitch, checked the Metro power once more, striking out the dangerous Krist on four pitched balls. Hightman, who had escaped a bad hole in the fifth by virtue of a two-ply killing, seemed laboring as he pitched to Jansky, starting off the Chiefs' half of the inning. Frank mentally checked the batting order. If Al got on, or either Eckert or Martsell did, Kelso was certain to pull Vanderpool out. His heart leaped when Jansky powdered a single through the middle.

Hightman nicked Eckert with an inside pitch after he had gotten ahead of the hitter, nothing and two, and the crowd caught the scent of New York blood when Martsell moved in to hit. Kelso had to get a hitter out there behind the right fielder, and quickly he called Vander-pool back as the second baseman left the dugout—and Frank was about to lift himself off the bench when Kelso singled out Pete Ibarra. "Get one of your old brand, Pete," he said. The second baseman up from the Steers made no attempt to hide his feelings, and his pantomime of impatience brought a dry smile to Kelso's face. "Right now, Hyatt," he fairly spat out, "we want a bass viol, not a banjo!"

"Play him or trade him, Sam," Hy Brown quipped, and mirth rippled the length of the dugout.

Frank, not exactly subdued, gritted his teeth and watched Martsell hang in against Hightman and run the count out full, only to loft easily to the Metro first base-man. The volume of sound in the stands tapered off, then swelled again when Ibarra threw his loaded bat away and carried his official war club to the first base side of the plate. Many of the fans remembered that Pete had hit forty-three homers for the Chiefs not too many seasons ago. A bad knee had hastened his decline.

The veteran slugger let a strike go by, then brought the crowd up howling when he creamed a fast ball to right, but the drive was foul by more than ten feet. Hightman got a new ball, rubbed it up, then caught the outside corner of the plate with a wicked breaking pitch, and Ibarra shook his head sadly as he walked back to the bench amid a storm of abuse from the fans. "Sam," he said to Kelso, "I'm too old to argue, but that pitch was down around my ankles. That O'Dea must have been a drop-out from umpire school."

"It looked good from here," the manager said, "Pete, you wouldn't look too bad in bifocals."

Frank had to fight off an almost uncontrollable urge to give Kelso that certain look that would have told him that maybe a banjo could have played louder music. The manager's voice suddenly shook him from head to heel, lifted him off the bench. "Take over at second base, Hyatt!" Kelso said, and turned to the lineup he had posted in the dugout to scratch off Vanderpool's name.

He lost no time getting out of the dugout to the infield, and while the public address system notified the crowd of the change, he smoothed out the dirt with his spikes and told himself it was time to take over, from Duhamel and everyone else. From now on he had to make himself noticed and kick the lantern out from under his bushel. Looking up he saw that the TV cameras were on him, and hoped the video screen in Tom Thorp's garage in Indiana would not be snowed in. From short, Ken Provost chirped at Jason Bozer, and Frank chimed in. "Throw him old 'Uncle Charlie,' Jase! Wind it around his neck!"

The Chief pitcher looked out at him as he took the shine off a fresh baseball. His grin was as wide as the plate. He did break the curve off to get a strike on the New York leadoff man, but his next offering, a fast ball, was sliced into right for a single. Kelso alerted his bullpen, but the firemen stopped throwing a few moments later when Frank cut to his right, flagged down a hot grounder and tossed to Provost, covering second. The shortstop's throw to Eckert completed the two-ply killing, and the crowd gave the play a solid reception.

Bozer, fighting control, walked two men in succession, and the Milwaukee relief pitchers got up to throw once more. Jansky came out to the mound, and the colored southpaw assured him he was all right but suggested that he take a good look at the umpire and see if he'd lost one of his contact lenses.

A wrong-side hitter at the plate, Frank shifted to his

179

left, and he was almost on the edge of the grass when the batter hit a short fly ball into right. He turned and ran under its high, lazy arc, and was aware of Martsell racing in. He heard the right fielder shout him off, but he had no intention of putting on the brakes for two good reasons—the first being that he was dead certain Martsell had no chance to get to the ball, the second and most important being that he was not going to be shunted aside any more. He spun half around, lunged, and got the ball in the webbing of his glove, his right shoulder slamming into Martsell and sending the outfielder sprawling. The impact dropped him five feet away but he held on to the ball.

When he got to his feet and discovered himself intact, Tom Shugrue and half a dozen Milwaukee players were moving in to determine the extent of damage. Ira Eckert yelled, "Showboat!" at him, and the intended uncomplimentary remark sounded like a barrel of praise.

He trotted in, the crowd giving him a great round of applause, and he was toweling the dirt and sweat from his face when Martsell came limping in to the dugout between the trainer and Joe Arriga. "It was *my* ball, you busher!" the right fielder thrust at him.

"I figured it was mine," Frank said. "Sue me!" He moved along to the water fountain and rinsed out his mouth, still enchanted by the roar in the stands he had touched off.

When he took his place on the bench, Richie Duhamel observed dryly, "We either need a traffic cop out there or more collision insurance."

Kelso came by and glared at Duhamel, then at Frank. "Yeah—monkey see, monkey do!"

Duhamel turned loose a small laugh. "Imitation is the sincerest flattery, Sam."

Kelso sent utility third baseman Joe Kustra up to hit for Bozer, and the crowd's excitement built up when he beat out a bunt just inside the first base line. It sagged When Ken Provost forced him at second, then rose again when Jonny Drew got a leg-hit to deep short. Hightman, sensing the hook, worked too fine on Raneri and loaded the bases. The Metro manager came out on his aged legs and held a conference with his battery, then decided to go along with Hightman. Joe Arriga, after running the string out, lifted a sky-high pop to the infield, leaving it up to Jansky to bring in the runs needed to tie or go ahead. The Metro pitcher, an iceberg when the going really got rough, reached back for that extra few ounces of effort and got two quick strikes over, moving the ball inside, then outside and getting the corners. He wasted a pitch, came in with a change-up that Jansky fouled off, then broke off another jug-handle curve that had the hitter looking. Hightman was leaving the mound even before the umpire made his call.

The fans, many of them heading for the exits, hooted at the Chiefs as they took the field, the lion's share of the razzing directed toward the Milwaukee catcher. Frank anticipated the pressure that would be on the lower part of Kelso's batting order when the Chiefs returned for their cuts, and he certainly hoped he had left a pair of rabbit ears back in the minors.

Ordway, Kelso's relief for Bozer, had his work cut out for him with Krist and Chagares, the cellar dwellers' one-two punch, starting things off. Frank went out close to the outfield grass, shifted far to his left, and was in perfect position to take Krist's screaming one-hopper and throw his man out. Chagares doubled into right, and Ordway walked the next hitter. Up in the stands the fans were still on the move. Half a dozen pitches later, Provost dug out a ground ball and fired to Frank, who rifled to Eckert, and the Metro threat was choked off.

Frank, running in, faced that moment of truth again, and the sweat on him turned a little cold. He knew he had been "good field" thus far, but there was only one way to make a hit with the fans, and that was to *hit*. He knew one thing. If Kelso sent a man up to hit for him he would break a bat over the manager's hard skull.

High up in the seats that horn tooted again and sent a shiver through him. Was it an omen, good or bad?

● SEVENTEEN

IT WAS THE LAST OF THE EIGHTH, WITH THE THIN PART
of the Milwaukee batting order due up, and many of the
fans were on the move when Ira Eckert stepped in to face
Hightman. With Martsell on deck, Frank watched Kelso
out of the corner of his eye and fought a battle with his
nerves. Hy Brown added to his agony when the reserve
outfielder got up and moved around. The Negro bent one
knee, then the other. He flexed his arms and said, "Man,
do I need a change of oil!" He sat down again, and
Frank let some breath out and concentrated on positive
thinking.

He watched Eckert work Hightman into a three and
one corner, then slam a hit through the middle. When
Martsell left the waiting station, Frank got up on legs that
started to shake and moved to the bat rack, and Kelso
barked, "What are you waitin' for, Hyatt? Get out there
with a stick!"

The distance to the on-deck circle seemed a country mile, and with each step he took he was afraid the manager would change his mind and call on the long ball hitter. He worked on the handle of his bat with the pine tar as Martsell grimly hung in against the Metro pitcher. The count full, he fouled three into the stands before he got the fourth ball. Frank swallowed hard to get his heart back into place as he moved toward the plate, and even before he dug in he was sickeningly aware of what Kelso's strategy would have to be. With two on and nobody out, he would be expected to push Eckert and Martsell around where they could score on any kind of a hit. Rebellion was having its way with him when he ignored Hightman's first pitch, a fast ball that was too high.

He looked up the line at the third base coach, hoping the sign might be taken off and that Kelso might have remembered he had a two-seventy hitter at the plate. No, he still had to lay one down. Give yourself up. Move the other guy along. That had been the story of his life—all that rugged way from a little strawberry patch in Indiana to this first official time at bat in the Milwaukee County Stadium. Begrudgingly he ran his hands up the bat handle when the next pitch came in, moved back when it looked too close inside, and had a strike called against him. The Metro pitcher was keeping his stuff high, and that was another source of temptation, for that was where he hit them best. He stepped out and scooped up some dirt, only vaguely aware of the exhortations from the crowd that remained, stone deaf to the riding from the visitors' bench.

Sure, there was a ball game at stake here, and so was a man's pride and a new image. He visualized one statistic in the box score in the morning paper. *S-Hyatt.* And maybe, considering the vagaries of life as he had known it and the baseball brass, that was all they would ever remember him by. The Metro first and third basemen were ready to creep in when Hightman got ready to throw again, and Frank knew he would gladly swap a year's salary for Kelso's go-ahead sign to drive the ball down one of their throats. All the frustrations, all the errors of omission in his past plagued him as he dropped his bat on Hightman's delivery that broke in under his knees. He held up in time and glared up the line at Kelso's traffic man.

He hung in there and worked a plainly tiring Hightman to three and one, and hopefully looked for the green light on the ball that had to come over. Kelso, however, was doing the thinking, weighing the possibility of his man hitting into a double play against a walk that would fill the bases. His order was to take, and steaming under his protective helmet, he left the batter's box and made his way to the on-deck circle to get rosin he did not need. What he did need was a little time to put down the rebellion against the man he had always been, one who always got out and pushed but seldom if ever found himself in the driver's seat.

Hy Brown, waiting to hit for the relief pitcher, Ordway, tossed him a grin with the rosin bag. "I know, man. It's a most temptin' spot, but don't get ideas, y' hear?"

The crowd's impatient roar slammed against his back as he retraced his steps. The Metro corner men, sure that the bunt sign was still on, edged in when Hightman stretched. This was the moment, as he took a foothold, when all those old years fell into focus, when familiar faces appeared up there in the lights, and voices sounded in his ears. "They like to save certain dishes for the regular customers, Frank. They'll push you around in this cockeyed world if you let 'em. You've got to assert your-self." Even as Hightman reared back and fired, he was wondering what had become of Hog Wilding.

It was a pitch he had always considered made to order. High and fast, and ready to nick the outside corner. He had to make up his mind in the next split second, was about to lay off when that fan high up in the stands let loose a blast from his horn. It was all the excuse he needed. He took a terrific cut, felt the impact of the ball meeting his bat clear up to his shoulders, and knew he had never hit one harder in his whole life. Rounding first, he watched the ball drop into the left field seats, fair by a good ten feet, and the fans were up and jumping and in full cry for the first time since the game began.

As he wheeled around third, the coach there caught at his outstretched hand, but the man's face was as hard as a rock. Eckert and Martsell waited for him at the plate, hurriedly offered congratulations, and seemed in a hurry to get clear of him. After the halfhearted reception from the bench, Frank turned to face a raging Sam Kelso.

"That'll cost you a hundred, Hyatt!" the manager roared above the noise still washing out of the stands, and then he began to sputter like bacon frying in a pan, at a loss to reach for his gamiest words. "Y-You fresh busher! You——!" He abruptly turned away, and yelled out at Hy Brown, who was trying to keep the rally alive against a new Metro pitcher.

Frank, feeling ten feet tall, dogged Kelso's steps. "If you had hit me for two hundred, Sam, I would have called it money in the bank. Sometime when you have three or four hours to spare, Sam, I'll tell you why I had to tie into that pitch. You've heard it before—a man does only what he has to do."

Kelso swung his head around. "Sure, so when I hand

186

you a pink slip and a bus ticket back to the boondocks, you remember that, Hyatt!"

"But this time I'll have something to take along with me, Sam." He went back to his place on the bench, followed by the manager's puzzled glance, and after watching Hy Brown sky deep to center, he got up and followed Richie Duhamel to the drinking fountain. "Shake a leg, Richie," he said. "The new man wants a drink."

The injured second baseman stepped aside. "Sure, Frank, be my guest."

Johnny Drew grounded out, and the Chiefs took the field with a 4-3 lead. Danny Sloat took over the pitching chores and retired three Metros in a row. On his way to the showers Frank was certain that Kelso would be all-forgiving, for he was a smart man and most certainly would have received a book on his new infielder from Bert Moger. He would agree that a man had to know when it was time to take himself over—with limitations, of course. In the dressing room a writer crowded him near his locker. "How do you feel after that one, Hyatt?"

"Fine, one hundred dollars," he said. "Please, you are in my way!" He chuckled deep down when the scribe mumbled his apology and took his leave. Looking into the mirror hanging inside his locker door, Frank stared at his image, and for the first time since he could remember, liked what he saw. He could hardly wait until it was time to show it to Tom Thorp.

Some day soon, he told himself under the shower, he would have to learn the identity of the man who blew that sour horn. Such a timely assist could not go unrewarded.

THE AUTHOR

JOE ARCHIBALD began his writing career at the age of fifteen with a prize-winning contribution to the *Boston Post*. At twelve, he had submitted and sold his first cartoon to the original *Judge* magazine. He is a graduate of the Chicago Academy of Fine Arts.

During World War I, he served on a U. S. Navy subchaser and was staff cartoonist for a service publication. After the armistice he was a police and sports reporter for Boston newspapers, and then became a sports and panel cartoonist for the McClure Newspaper Syndicate in New York. Free-lancing since 1929, he has written countless stories and articles for boys on sports, aviation and adventure. With the outbreak of World War II, Joe Archibald became a cartoonist for the American Theatre Wing, and went overseas as a field director for the Red Cross.

His first book, published in 1947, won for him an enthusiastic following of young readers throughout the country, and the books he has written since then have proved his popularity with sportsminded boys.

He is a member of the National Cartoonist Society, has exhibited water colors, and is a director of amateur musical shows. He lives in Port Chester, New York, and is very active in community affairs.